D0055638

The Dog in the Wood

The Dog in the Wood

MONIKA SCHRÖDER

FRONT STREET
Honesdale, Pennsylvania

Printed in the United States of America
Designed by Helen Robinson
First edition
Second printing

Library of Congress Cataloging-in-Publication Data

Schröder, Monika.
The dog in the wood / Monika Schröder. — 1st ed.
p. cm.
Summary: As World War II draws to an end, Russian soldiers occupy Schwartz, Germany, bringing both friendship and hardship to the family of ten-year-old Fritz, whose grandfather was a Nazi sympathizer, eventually forcing them to leave their farm, then arresting Fritz's mother and her hired hand.
ISBN 978-1-59078-701-4 (hardcover : alk. paper)
1. Germany—History—1933–1945—Juvenile fiction. 2. World War, 1939–1945—Juvenile fiction. [1. Germany—History—1933–1945—Fiction. 2. World War, 1939–1945—Fiction. 3. Family life—Germany—Fiction. 4. Farm life—Germany—Fiction. 5. Russians—Germany—Fiction. 6. Political prisoners—Fiction.] I. Title.
PZ7.S37955Dog 2009
[Fic]—dc22 2009004970

FRONT STREET
An Imprint of Boyds Mills Press, Inc.
815 Church Street
Honesdale, Pennsylvania 18431

(*Für meinen Vater*)

The Dog in the Wood

1

In the distance Fritz heard again the droning of engines. The front was coming closer, and the east wind blew the noise of cannons, tanks, and gunfire toward their farm. The Russians would be there soon. Fritz set down the tray with the tomato seedlings on the corner post of the garden fence and looked up into the cloudless sky. No sign of the Luftwaffe. The Russians should have come during the winter when the weather was gloomy and everyone had to stay inside. Now, in late April, Fritz enjoyed being outside and the best time for gardening had begun. The garden was at the south end of the farm, behind the barn, overlooking the pond and the family's forest in the distance. Fritz imagined the Russians coming through the forest. Would they arrive in tanks? Would there be air raids? He had seen a picture of a Russian soldier in a leaflet about Bolshevism on Grandpa's desk. A man with a shorn head and mean eyes, holding a knife between his teeth, was running after a blond child. Fritz squatted down and began his work. Better not to think about what would happen when the Russians arrived. He loosened the fragile tomato seedlings from their pots and set them one by one into the row of small hollows he had prepared in the soil. By the time the tomatoes were ripe the war would be long over.

Grandpa still believed in the German victory. But fewer and fewer people seemed to share his conviction. In recent weeks, most villagers had gone back to saying simply "Good Day" when they met Grandfather on the street instead of returning his "Heil Hitler" greeting. Grandpa owned the largest farm in the village. At the main entrance a sign in bold letters under a swastika announced him as the head of the local Nazi Party Farmers' Association.

Last weekend, as Fritz had helped Oma Lou pluck feathers off a chicken, Grandpa had come home from a meeting in his uniform and thrown his hat on the coat rack, entering the kitchen with his big ears flaming red.

"What's the matter, Karl?" Oma Lou had asked, looking up. "Why are you upset?"

"People are showing their real colors. The end is near," Grandfather had answered. "They are beginning to hang their coats in the new wind."

Fritz had imagined all the neighbors in colorful new coats, taking them off and letting them blow in the wind. But the worried expression on Oma Lou's face had told him he had misunderstood his grandfather's comment, and he had been left wondering what it meant.

Grandpa thought that gardening was women's work, but Fritz loved to care for Oma Lou's large garden. He had germinated these tomatoes and put them into small earthen pots on the windowsill in the hallway. Now that the small plants had each grown at least five leaves, they were ready to be planted in the garden. Tomatoes need sunshine, and here, along the fence at the south end of the garden, they would be fully exposed to the afternoon light.

"Don't waste your time with tomatoes, boy!" Grandpa's voice suddenly boomed from the other side of the fence. "Come with me!"

Fritz still needed to water the plants, but Grandpa was already striding back to the house. Fritz hurried to follow Grandpa's orders. He shook the dirt off his pants and left the garden tools at the side of the fence, wondering which chore Grandpa would assign him now. When he entered the yard, Grandpa had taken his seat on the horse cart and was motioning Fritz to climb up next to him.

"Where are we going?" Fritz asked as Grandpa stirred the horses toward the forest.

"I want to show you something," Grandpa replied. The edge of the woods grew closer, and when they reached the low fir trees marking the entrance to the family's forest, Grandpa stopped the horses and stepped down from the seat of the cart. "We'll leave the horses here and walk the last part."

Fritz jumped off and followed Grandpa into the woods.

"Come on, boy!" Grandpa called now, and hurried briskly through the underbrush. Fritz had to rush to follow Grandpa's long stride. Grandpa's presence seemed to leave less space in his chest to breathe. He was panting when Grandpa finally stopped in front of a large pine tree. Several cut branches were spread out flat under the tree. Grandpa bent down to move one of the branches aside. A large rectangular hole, about five feet deep, came into view. Fresh soil was piled up behind the tree trunk. "Did you dig this hole?" Fritz looked into the dugout. The old man nodded. "What is it for?" A large vein was throbbing on Grandpa's neck. Fritz had seen the throbbing vein before. It seemed to bulge before Grandpa broke out into a fit of rage. A quick surge of guilt shot through Fritz, but he didn't have enough time to search his mind for what he might be guilty of.

"This will be the hideout for your mother, your grandmother, and your sister when the Russians reach our village." Fritz imagined Mama; his sister, Irmi; and Oma Lou huddled inside the hole while Russian soldiers searched the forest.

"Now see if there is enough space for three people." Grandpa took the rope he had brought, tied one end around the tree beside the hole, and passed Fritz the other end. Fritz, still taken by the image of the women hidden in the hole while Russians were shooting from behind trees, just stared. He wanted to ask why space for just three people was all that was needed, but his throat was too tight to speak. Grandpa nudged him to climb down into the hole. Reluctantly, he lowered himself along the rope into the opening.

"You and I will defend our land against the Bolshevik enemy," Grandpa declared as if he had read Fritz's mind. Fritz shuddered in the cool dampness that surrounded him. How could the two of them defend their farm against the approaching Russian army? Fritz had turned ten only last month. He pictured himself with a large rifle standing beside Grandpa, firing against the approaching enemy soldiers. The Russians were supposed to be fierce and cruel fighters. Fritz took hold of the rope, looking up to see if he had permission to climb back up again.

"I want you to know where to find the women in case something happens to me," Grandpa called down. "This pine tree will be your landmark. It's easy to recognize. It's taller than the others, and its trunk splits into two arms. You see?" Grandpa pointed toward the treetop. "It looks like a fork." Fritz followed Grandpa's arm, still trying to make sense of what he had just heard. Down in the hole Fritz felt even smaller and weaker than when he stood beside Grandpa. What did Grandpa mean when he said "if something happens to me ..."? Was Grandpa expecting to die in the fight for the village?

"What about Lech?" Fritz dared to ask, but his voice

came out like a croak. If they had to fight, Fritz wanted to be close to Lech.

"That Polack will probably run away soon. The two French laborers at the Bartels' farm ran away last week, taking a horse with them. You don't need to worry about the Pole once the Russians come." Grandpa dismissed Fritz's worry with a quick movement of his hand, throwing a birdlike shadow over the hole.

"But he has worked for us for a long time. Couldn't he help us?" The words came out more softly than Fritz had wanted.

"These forced laborers didn't come here because they wanted to work for us. We made them come here." Grandpa stepped close to the hole. The tip of his left boot loomed over the rim.

"Stomp down the soil for a floor," Grandpa ordered before Fritz could ask how he was so sure that Lech wanted to run away. Lech was tall and strong, and he could be helpful defending the farm. Small rivulets of sandy soil slid down the sides while Fritz tamped the ground with his shoes. "Tomorrow we'll bring some boards to hold up the sides and to protect the hole from rain."

"How long will they have to stay in here?"

"We don't know," Grandpa said, his voice less audible because he spoke in the direction of the treetops. Then, with a quick gesture, Grandpa signaled Fritz to come back up.

"Does Grandma have to climb in and out with this rope?" Fritz asked as he scrambled out.

"No. I will bring a small ladder." Grandpa rolled up the rope and swung it over his shoulder. "Let's go back."

When they reached the horse cart at the forest's edge, Grandpa threw the rope into the cart and climbed back onto the seat. The horses' ears twitched attentively, and their large eyes followed the old man's movements. Fritz saw himself running through the forest frantically trying to find the tall forked pine tree while Russians were jumping from behind the bushes. His heartbeat quickened as he turned around to see if he could make out the tree from a distance.

"Come on, boy. I'm already late for my meeting with the other farmers. Tomorrow is the führer's birthday, and we are planning a small celebration. I also have to talk to the men about our plan to defend the village," Grandpa said.

Fritz pulled himself up and took his seat beside Grandpa on the horse cart. "How much longer will it be until the front reaches us, Grandpa?"

"The last time a German army jeep came through we were told that the front was now about thirty kilometers away. That means it could be less than a week before they'll reach us here in Schwartz. We have to get ready for the last battle for our homeland." Grandpa's voice sounded as if he were giving a speech to a larger audience. “No worries, boy. The German spirit will prevail!” Grandpa boomed. Fritz nodded but wondered if Grandpa himself believed his own words as he clutched the reins so hard that white crescents appeared under the tops of his fingernails. Fritz knew there was reason to worry.

Grandpa stopped the horses in front of their gate. “You go inside, Fritz. I’ll be home for dinner soon. Don’t forget! The dugout has to remain a secret between the two of us. I don’t want to tell the women about it yet.”

2

As Fritz entered the house, his worries about the hole dissolved in the sweet aroma wafting from the oven. It was Friday, Fritz's favorite day, when Oma Lou baked bread and sheet cake. He loved it so much that sometimes in the evening when he went to bed, before he put his clothes over the back of the chair, he would hold his shirt close to his nose to take in a last whiff of cake.

"Well, you came too late to lick the bowl," Oma Lou said. "But maybe I'll let you try some of the warm cake." She ruffled his hair in passing before continuing to dry a wooden spoon.

His sister, Irmi, walked in. "Where were you all afternoon?" she asked. "I thought you where supposed to help us with the wash." Irmi was four years older than Fritz and acted as if she were a second mother to him. Her pigtails whipped as she turned to Fritz, expecting an answer.

"Grandpa asked me to help him," Fritz said, hoping she would not press him to lie by asking for more details.

Mama entered the kitchen with a small dried sausage

from the pantry. She looked exhausted, and her hair was flat and dull. She hadn't taken the time to part and comb it neatly into the style he liked. Fritz waited for Mama to comment on the row of tomato seedlings he had planted in the garden, but instead she said, "Fritz, go get the butter from the cellar." He was disappointed that she hadn't noticed, but these were hard times for Mama. She was arguing with Grandpa most evenings. Fritz wished he could tell her about the hole, but he wouldn't disobey Grandpa's order to keep it a secret.

Fritz walked to the mudroom connecting the hallway with the covered porch that led to the backyard. Here they stored their boots, overcoats, brooms, and the aluminum bathtub. Large enamel bowls hung from hooks on the wall, and the back wall was covered with shelves of jars containing canned fruits and pickled vegetables. Fritz bent down to open the wooden door to the cellar stairs. A musty odor wafted up. As he carefully stepped down into the darkness, the smell reminded him of the secret hole Grandpa had shown him that afternoon. Would they have enough time to take food? Should he take some food to the dugout now in preparation? Grandma would worry about the farm animals. He imagined Irmi crying. If Mama let him stay back to fight with Grandpa, he needed to learn how to shoot. He had gone hunting with Grandpa but without ever killing anything. On a side shelf he found the butter wrapped in moist waxed paper and carried it upstairs.

In the kitchen Fritz again inhaled the smell of the

cake, which had now been placed under the window to cool. He handed Mama the butter, and in return she passed him two buckets, which he knew contained food scraps mixed with boiled potato skins for the pigs. It was Irmi's turn to feed the pigs, but Fritz wouldn't complain. Mama didn't like it when they argued.

In the pigsty he watched the pigs pushing and shoving with their pink snouts as they each tried to reach the food first, accompanied by excited squeals and grunts. *They* didn't feel any tension about the approaching Russians. Soon the squealing gave way to a chorus of contented smacking. He washed out the buckets and cleaned his hands at the water pump in the yard before returning to the house.

As usual they had a cold dinner. As on other days, the warm meal of the day had been eaten at noon. On the table was bread with butter, salami, and cheese. Grandfather entered the room with a solemn expression on his face. "How was your meeting, Karl?" Oma Lou asked, passing the bread basket to him.

"We need to plan for the defense of the village. The Russians have broken through the lines at Fürstenberg. Now it can only be a matter of days until they reach us. I talked to the village elders today, but many don't want to defend the village." Grandpa spoke hastily, as if out of breath.

"What do they want?" Mama looked up while placing a slice of bread on her plate.

"They want us to surrender!" Grandpa responded, cutting a thick slice of the salami. "Werner Güntzel thinks it is best to hang out white flags." The sentence hovered over the dinner table. A fly was caught in the curtain; its sizzling filled the silence. Fritz remembered the drawing of the fierce-looking man with the mean eyes. He pictured a battalion of them holding their rifles and marching down the village road.

"We need to build obstacles to hinder the tanks from entering the village." Grandpa Karl was talking louder than necessary. "Everyone should be out digging trenches to fight the tanks. We need to put logs on the roads to slow them down. People should dig hide-outs in the forest to shelter women and children."

The vein was pulsing on Grandpa Karl's neck. Fritz looked away. Now they would begin their argument again.

"What good does that do?" Mama spoke up. "I'm not going to hide in the woods. How can you defend the village when the German army has been forced to retreat before the Russians? How many more people have to die?" She took a deep breath. "The war is over. The Americans have crossed the Elbe River, and the Russians are in Berlin. It'll be only days until they reach us. We are protected by the forest and the lakes, but they will soon be here as well." Oma Lou shot a pleading glance at Mama, wishing to avoid the looming argument, but Mama continued. "Even our own soldiers are fleeing from the front. Gerda Schreiber saw a group of German deserters the other day on her way to the mill." Mama's face was flushed, and she rubbed her thumb over her fingertips the way she did when she was nervous. If Papa were here, he might be able to help Mama to convince Grandpa. But his father had died in the first year of the war. Fritz was only four years old then, and he barely remembered his father's face.

"We owe it to the nation to defend ourselves!" Grandpa declared resolutely. "We cannot surrender to the Bolsheviks!" Small pearls of sweat collected on his forehead. The old man used the back of his huge hand to swipe it off. "We cannot just give up!" he blustered, pushing his chair back and leaving the kitchen, taking his plate with him.

"Let him be!" Oma Lou pleaded.

"Let *him* be. He doesn't let *us* be! That's the problem!" Mama shook her head and took another bite from her bread. Fritz looked at his sister. Irmi began to cry. He forced himself to take another bite from his half-eaten sandwich. Mama, still chewing, bent across the table and squeezed Irmi's hand.

"I'm so afraid. What are they going to do to us?" Irmi sobbed. Fritz wished she would stop right now.

"It'll be all right. Don't worry," Mama said, swallowing. "We don't have anything they want."

"But I heard Erna Seiler talk about what they are doing to women and girls. She heard it from a woman who fled from the East. They put a girl in a …" Irmi was now dissolving in tears. Fritz wanted to run outside. Why couldn't she keep quiet? It was hard to breathe in the kitchen, but he was not allowed to leave the dinner table before everyone was finished.

"It will be all right," Oma Lou said, wringing her hands helplessly. "The Almighty will protect us!" Oma Lou hardly ever mentioned God, and the family seldom attended church. Hearing her mention God now was more alarming than comforting.

Mama and Oma Lou exchanged worried looks. Fritz wiped his mouth with the back of his right hand, leaving a glistening smear on his skin. He forced himself to take the last bite from his sandwich. The bread tasted like paper. He took a sip of milk to make swallowing easier.

"Would anyone like a piece of sheet cake?" Oma Lou asked. But they had all lost their appetites, and Mama started to collect the dishes. Fritz felt bad to turn down Oma Lou's offer, but he needed to get up and move around. He returned the butter to the cellar. Irmi washed her face at the kitchen sink.

From the living room they could hear the sound of the radio. After a long high-pitched static squeak, classical music flowed from the brown receiver. Fritz was drying the dishes when the familiar voice of Joseph Goebbels, Hitler's minister of propaganda, began a speech honoring the führer's birthday. Dramatically, he affirmed Germany's final victory and thanked Hitler in the name of the German nation. Due to the static Fritz could not understand everything, but he picked up the words "heroes" and "infamy of the enemy." Goebbels continued, "Within a few years after the war Germany will flourish as never before. Its ruined landscapes and provinces will be filled with new, more beautiful cities and villages." Oma Lou shook her head and turned to join her husband in the living room. Fritz put the last plate back into the cupboard. Mama removed her apron and hung it on a nail close to the door.

"They don't know what they are saying anymore. The Nazis have lost. They just don't know it yet. It's time for peace."

3

Grandpa Karl didn't let Lech sit at the family table, so Mama had Fritz take his meals out to the barn. Fritz was glad to see Lech. Since Lech had come to work for the family last summer, Fritz had grown close to the big, burly Pole. Lech sat at his workbench in the barn, holding a piece of wood under a light. In his spare time he carved figures out of soft wood.

"Hmm! My dinner." Lech turned around and cleared the workbench for Fritz to put down his plate. "Thank you!"

Lech didn't have much hair on his head, but his arms were covered with reddish curls, and a ring of the same curls circled his head.

"You look like three days of rain, Fritz. What's the matter?" He scrunched his face into a mock frown, sending a ripple of small wrinkles onto his strong nose and over his freckled forehead. Lech's funny grimace usually made Fritz laugh, but today he couldn't even smile.

"They were arguing again. Grandpa Karl wants to fight the Russians," Fritz said, sitting down on the bench next to Lech. "And Mama says that he shouldn't."

"Your mother is right." Lech took a large bite out of the bread and chewed off a bite from the cheese. "Even the German army couldn't stop the Russians. That's why they will be here soon."

"Grandpa wants me to go with him and take a rifle."

"You'd better stay away."

"But I have to do what he says. Maybe I should practice shooting," Fritz said, imagining himself again fighting Russians with Grandpa.

"No you shouldn't," Lech said, finishing the first slice of bread. Fritz wished he could tell Lech about the hole, but a secret was a secret.

"Maybe you could come with me?" Fritz asked.

"With you and your grandpa? I don't think your grandpa will trust me to defend his farm against the enemy." Lech nudged Fritz. "Don't worry about shooting at Russians. Your mother won't let you."

"But the Russians will come soon. What *will* happen?"

"We'll wait and see. They will be here any day now. They will come, and then they will go on to meet the Americans and British in Berlin." Lech gave Fritz's shoulder a quick squeeze. "It's like when a boat meets a storm. There will be broken water for a while, and then things will calm down."

"*Choppy* waters, not *broken*," Fritz corrected. He had helped Lech improve his German, but Lech often confused words. Fritz wondered if he did it on purpose, just to make him laugh.

"Okay then, choppy waters," Lech said. "But you know what I mean?"

Fritz nodded, hoping that it would be just a short storm.

"But you know what? I speak some Russian." Lech smiled at him. "I'm from eastern Poland, from an area that used to belong to the Ukraine. The Ukrainian language is very close to Russian."

Fritz remembered the map on his schoolroom's wall. Ukraine was a big country, part of the Soviet Union, bordering the Black Sea, a place the Nazis had wanted to take over.

"So you can ask them what they want. That's good." Fritz felt a little lighter.

"And now you should pass me the small carving knife over there, the one with the green handle." Lech pushed the plate away and turned his attention back to the piece of wood he was working on when Fritz had entered the barn.

"What are you making?"

"I'm still working on the old couple." Lech was carving two figures standing side by side. The man was wearing overalls. The woman was dressed in a peasant skirt and blouse. Lech took the carving knife Fritz passed him and with a few swift movements gave her face an aged expression.

"You are making her old," Fritz said.

"They *are* old."

Lech motioned toward the lump of wood that Fritz had been trying to shape into a dog. "Why don't you work on your dog?"

"My dog looks more like a pig without a neck." Fritz held the lump of wood in his hands. He would never be able to make it look like a dog.

"The dog is already there."

"Where?"

"Inside the piece of wood." Lech passed Fritz a carving knife and motioned him to start working.

"I don't see it."

"Not yet. But it's already there inside. You just need to uncover it."

4

Mama had just stretched out on the sofa for her Sunday afternoon nap when they heard knocking on the front door. It was Fritz's friend Paul.

"How did you get away from watching your little brother?" Fritz asked.

"Thomas is taking care of him today, so I'm free. Let's go to the main road!"

"My mother won't let me go that far anymore," Fritz answered. "Last week old Herr Heimann told her that an escaped French forced laborer had shot a peasant woman from a jeep as she was working in her field."

"So we just don't tell where we're going!" Paul answered. They heard Mama calling from the living room and followed her call.

"*Guten Tag*, Frau Friedrich. Can Fritz come out and play?"

"Where are you going to play?"

"We'll go out behind the wheat field and play with a ball," Paul said. The lie came easily from Paul's lips. Fritz quickly told himself that it was Paul who had said they were going to play ball.

Mama nodded. "Just be back in time."

Fritz grabbed his jacket, and Paul threw him a triumphant smile as they walked out the door. "Don't be a worrywart!" Paul teased him. "Nobody will find out unless you tell them." When they crossed the yard, a group of hens scurried away. Paul kicked a pebble after the slowest one.

The cow pastures at the south end of the village had been plowed into beet fields, and the green crowns of the plants spread out in rows across the dark soil. The weather had been blustery this spring, but now, after a rain shower, the sky was brilliant and the earth seemed cleaned up for Sunday. When they came to the end of the sugar beets, they turned right and made their way into the wheat field. Through it was a shortcut to the main road connecting their village with the county seat.

Last winter, the road had been filled with horse-drawn wagons and people on foot, all headed west. Trek after trek had clattered down the road. After Fritz had watched the treks the first time, Lech had explained that the refugees came from eastern Prussia and other German regions in the East. The people had all been fleeing from the Russians. Now they saw a trek only occasionally. There was also military traffic to watch.

Paul led the way up a nearby hillock. At first there was only the occasional truck, a jeep, or a horse cart on the road. Then Paul called out, "There's one coming."

The treks usually consisted of groups of refugees

from one village who were trying to stay together on their journey west. This one was made up of about eight wagons, led by a boy on a bicycle who rode ahead to scout out the way and to seek villages that were able and willing to take in refugees for the night. Some wagons rolled on big balloon tires pulled by strong farm horses and led by women in handsome coats. Others were just rickety carts, dragged along by a single mule or a shaggy-looking horse. Most wagons were covered with canvas, some with Oriental rugs. People packed onto the carts as many belongings as they could carry. All of them were fleeing without their fathers, of course, since the men were fighting in the war or had been killed. Some older men, probably grandfathers, were sitting on the carts or walking slowly beside their belongings. Had these grandfathers first tried to defend their villages? Fritz caught a glimpse of a boy sitting on a wooden box, steadying a clock in the crook of his right arm each time the wagon rolled over a stone or hole.

"Look at that." Paul pointed in the direction of a middle-aged woman who walked beside a scrawny horse, leading it on a rope. She turned around frequently, looking at the mare. Two big leather suitcases were tied onto its saddle, swaying with every step.

"What's wrong with the horse?" Fritz asked.

"I don't know. It looks very skinny," Paul answered.

"It also looks very sick," Fritz added, examining the shivering animal.

The horse was now stumbling, and its forelegs buckled every time its weight shifted. Then the horse stopped, and when the woman tried to pull it to the side of the road, it staggered into the ditch and fell on its side. The suitcases slid off the saddle. The boys saw the horse's belly heaving. It let out a heavy groan. The other people in the trek hardly took notice. Some looked briefly at the woman, but her place in line was quickly filled, and the group moved on. The horse moaned again. Then, with a last sigh, it leaned its head back, and a final shiver rippled through its emaciated body. The woman collapsed over it and cried.

"It just died," Paul stated.

Fritz wished that someone with a stronger horse would offer help to the old woman.

"What's she going to do now, I wonder," Fritz said. "She's all alone." Fritz looked at Paul, expecting an answer, but Paul just shrugged.

"Don't you feel bad for her?"

"She should have taken a stronger horse," Paul said.

The woman picked up the suitcases. With slumped shoulders she walked slowly, trying to catch up with the others.

"I want to go home now," Fritz said.

"All right, but let's come back soon."

"I'm not sure that we can," Fritz said as they began their way back. "My grandpa says the Russians will be here any day." Fritz looked back at the road. This is where Russian tanks would roll soon. German jeeps and soldiers would be fleeing. He could almost hear the gunshots and the roaring of the treads. He picked up a round stone from the path. "What will your family do when the Russians come?"

"My mother says we will put out a red flag and greet the Russians with food," Paul answered.

"Give them food? They are our enemies!" Fritz cried out.

"My mother can't wait until the Russians liberate us," Paul said.

"Liberate us from what?"

"From the Nazis, the brown pest! They brought all this on," Paul said. "My dad will come back once they free all the political prisoners. The Russians are Communists themselves, just like my dad."

Paul turned to Fritz. "What's *your* family going to do when the war is over?"

"My mother says it's time for peace. She says the Nazis lost, but they don't know it yet."

"What does your grandpa say?"

"He wants to defend the village," Fritz answered, smoothing his thumb over the stone.

"How? Karl Friedrich, the hero of Schwartz, the savior of the *Reich*?" Paul added.

"But what about all the horrible things the Russians have done to people?" Fritz now squeezed the stone in his fist.

"My mother says that the Russians will bring peace. That's what the Communists want."

"Haven't you seen the pictures? The fires in Dresden and Hamburg?" Fritz remembered the weekly newsreel film he had seen in a movie theater in Nirow. The Allied air raids had left big German cities destroyed. Mama had cried when she left the movie hall.

"What do you think German soldiers did in Russia?" Paul asked.

"What do you mean?"

"The German army invaded Russia without having been attacked. Now the Russians are defeating the Nazis. Their time has come." Paul was now slashing the long grass on the right side of the path, moving his hand like a scythe. "You have to pay a price when you lose a war."

Fritz wondered what Paul meant by that but did not dare to comment. Instead he asked, "What about your patriotic duty?"

"Hah!" Paul stopped. They had reached the edge of the village. "Patriotic duty! That's what your grandpa tells you. Are you his parrot?"

"No!" Fritz screamed. He wished he would know what to say, but he drew a blank. He hurled the stone into the field. Paul had started walking in the direction of his house.

5

Oma Lou was preparing dinner in the kitchen when Fritz returned to the house. She took a large loaf of bread out of the bread box, held it to her chest, cut off thick slices, and placed them in a small basket.

"Where have you been all afternoon?" she asked.

"Paul and I saw another refugee trek near Buschof," he answered, looking at her to check if she disapproved.

"More and more people are coming from the East. I don't know where they all are going to live." Oma Lou sighed.

"Do you think we are also going to leave Schwartz, Oma Lou?" Fritz asked, thinking of the dark stream of people and carts rolling slowly westward.

"Oh no! Your Grandpa and I are never going to live anywhere else." Oma Lou placed the bread basket on the table.

"But how can Grandpa defend the village?"

Oma Lou fastened a strand of her hair back into her bun. "There will be very tough times ahead once the war is over," she said, her voice low. She looked down and shook her head. "But leaving our home? Never! We don't know anyone in the West." She said what Fritz had hoped to hear. They wouldn't leave the farm. But the sadness in her voice made it impossible for him to feel relieved.

That night Fritz could not fall asleep. He again thought of the hole in the forest and tried to imagine how he and his grandpa would fight the Russians. He knew he would fail Grandpa. Paul's words also echoed in his head. Paul was so sure of everything, and he never seemed afraid. From the front room Fritz could hear the adults talking and the radio announcer warning the German people that "a grave and important announcement" was about to be made. Classical music followed. Then a man introduced himself as Grand Admiral Karl Dönitz, commander in chief for the north of Germany. Fritz strained his ears but could not hear the words. He got up and tiptoed into the hall, putting his ear close to the living room door. In somber tones, the man announced the death of Hitler and his own succession as führer of the *Reich*. Hitler had "fallen" that afternoon, he said, fighting "at the head of his troops."

"Oh, God!" he heard Oma Lou exclaim. "Lord help us! What are they going to do to us?"

"Let's get a white sheet and hang it out on the flagpole," he heard Mama say.

"How dare you say this, Gertrude?" Grandfather boomed. "The führer gave his life for us!"

"Karl, not so loud!" whispered Oma Lou. "The children are sleeping."

"We need to fight the Russians!" Grandpa's voice was lower now.

"How?" Mama replied. "There aren't even enough able men to do the farm work. Do you want the women and children to defend Schwartz against the Russian army? Why don't you realize that it's over? We don't need any more death and destruction. I have two children to care for. Germany has lost the war! Now we can only hope for a new beginning."

Fritz heard a deep sigh, then slow sobbing.

"Karl!" Oma Lou called out, alarmed.

"It's over!" Grandpa sobbed.

6

At first he only saw their shoes.

Oma Lou's were hanging a little higher than Grandpa's heavy black shoes. A thin wedge of morning light came in from the window in the barn roof, illuminating the swastika stitched onto Grandfather's right sleeve. For a moment it seemed as if the patch gave off the light itself. Grandpa's suit looked as it had when hanging in the bedroom closet after it had been pressed. A dark stain, shaped like a spoon, grew along Oma Lou's left stocking. Rope connected each neck to a broad beam above, the heads slightly cocked to one side, reminding Fritz of his hand puppets. Then, suddenly, he realized what he was seeing.

Fritz tried to breathe, but the air in the barn had turned thick. He needed to suck it through his nostrils in small portions.

Just as he took a step forward, he heard Mama's cry from behind. She grabbed him, her hands covering his eyes. As she pulled him closer, he could smell the onions she had cut for dinner the night before. Her hands felt cool and moist from the tears she had wiped from her face. Fritz squeezed his eyes shut and pushed his face against her hands, as if by pressing hard he could erase the image he had just seen.

"Fritz! Let's go inside!" Fritz made his legs move. When they stepped out of the barn, he was blinded for a second by the glare of sunlight flooding the yard. Mama led him inside to the living room sofa, and they sat side by side. She turned her face toward him, her eyes red and swollen.

"Why did they do this?" Fritz asked.

"Your Grandpa Karl was a very proud man," Mama began. "He lost his belief in Germany, I guess." She shook her head and looked at Fritz.

Fritz kept his eyes straight on Mama to keep the dark spot on Oma Lou's stocking from coming back into his mind. He needed to hear Mama's voice now, wanted to understand.

"Grandpa Karl was worried about what would happen after the war was lost. He was afraid he would lose all he had here in Schwartz. The last weeks have been very difficult for him." Even though he now closed his eyes, Fritz saw Grandpa hanging stiffly from the beam. He remembered his loud voice when he had told Fritz about the German victory and how he and Fritz would fight the Russians. Now Fritz wouldn't have to fight with Grandpa against the Russians. But there was no relief, just a pang of guilt.

"But what about Oma Lou?" Fritz swallowed hard. A salty taste crawled up his throat.

"The two of them had been married for forty years. I don't think she would have wanted to live without him."

"You are living without Papa for many years," Fritz replied.

"Yes, but your father was killed in the war and left me with two small children. It is a different situation. I have to take care of you and your sister." Mama gave a faint smile and squeezed his shoulder. "We'll stick together and get through this." She bent over and placed a kiss on his forehead. "Things will get better." He squeezed her hand harder.

7

Lech was nailing together a casket when Fritz entered the barn. Mama had left to find Irmi who was delivering cream to the neighbors. Lech put down his hammer and walked over to the other side of the workbench, sat down, and patted the space beside him.

"Is this for Oma?" Fritz asked and imagined Oma Lou lying on the bottom of the large casket, stiff as a doll in a drawer.

"No, this is the casket for your grandpa. We'll bury your grandma in her old dowry chest." Lech put his arm around Fritz's shoulder and pulled him closer. Fritz leaned his cheek against the leathery back of Lech's hand.

"Your Oma Louise was a good woman," Lech said. "But she is probably better off where she is now." Fritz was not sure about that, but he wanted Lech to keep talking. Hearing Lech's voice and feeling the weight of his arm around his shoulders helped slow down the spinning images in his head. Fritz imagined how the caskets would be buried side by side in the village cmetery.

"Were they so afraid of the Russians? Is that why

they did this?" Fritz asked. Lech took a deep breath before he answered.

"Well, your grandpa wore the uniform with the swastika. He was worried about what would happen to him after the Russians came."

Fritz, once again, saw Grandpa Karl under that pine tree, showing him the hole. "I want you to know where it is in case something happens to me," Grandpa had said. Had Grandpa known that he wouldn't be there when the Russians came? Fritz wanted to tell Lech about the hole. Was there a point in keeping a dead person's secret?

Lech leaned forward and turned to look at Fritz's face.

"Hey," Lech said, shaking Fritz gently. "It's going to be all right."

Fritz nodded. But there was one more thing he wanted to ask. "Will you go back home now that the war is over?" Fritz held his breath for a moment, afraid of the answer.

"No, I think I'll stick around for a while," he said, turning to Fritz with a big smile. "I like it here, and before I had to leave my village my brother and I had a big fight. We used to run a farm together, but then he wanted me out. Even if I went back to Poland, there wouldn't be anything to go back to." He paused. "I think your mother can use some help, and I still need to teach you how to carve."

Fritz turned to give Lech a hug. Lech embraced Fritz with his strong arms, and as he pressed his face against Lech's shoulder, Fritz felt less frightened of what was to come.

8

No one had thought of the asparagus. The night before, Fritz had peeked under the cloth that covered the mounds of sand in which the asparagus grew. It was ready to harvest. Fritz shivered in the morning cold. He had brought with him a basket, a dishcloth, and a knife. Asparagus had to be cut at dawn to prevent the stalks from turning dark. He gently moved the soil from the tips, dug the knife deep along the stem, and cut the tender stalks. Fritz collected the spears in his basket and covered them with a kitchen towel to block out light. Fritz liked the cracking sound of his knife cutting the stalks, and he was looking forward to the prepared asparagus he would eat later. Oma used to call asparagus the "king of vegetables." He cut two rows, filling the basket to its rim. When he returned to the kitchen, Mama and Irmi were having breakfast. He put the basket on the table, beaming at Mama. Mama lifted the dishcloth and burst out, "Oh no. The asparagus!" Fritz didn't understand. Her tone of voice didn't match the reaction he had expected. He stared at her. Mama swallowed, then with a softer voice said,

"Fritz, we don't have time to prepare it. They say that the Russians will be here today. We need to get ready."

"I'll peel it," Fritz said, looking down. "Then you just have to steam it."

"All right." Mama sighed, and mussed his hair.

After lunch Mama opened the sideboard and took out Grandfather Karl's watch and all his Nazi lapel pins. "We should have burned these together with his uniforms," she mumbled, placing all the items into a small box.

Irmi sat on the sofa, cutting the chevrons off her Young Maiden uniform.

"What if they nail us to the wall? That's what I heard from one of the refugees." Irmi's voice took on the hysterical note Fritz hated. "Or take us to Siberia? We cannot just stay here and wait."

"We don't have any other option," Mama said. "What could they possibly want from us?"

Fritz wondered if he should mention the hole to Mama now. They still had enough time to reach it.

"I don't want to just sit here and wait!" Irmi said in a voice shrill with fear.

"Well, if we had wanted to join the refugee treks, we should have done it much earlier. Now we'll stay here and await whatever happens." Mama picked up the box and walked toward the living room door. "I'll take this box up to the attic. Fritz, can you open the door, please?"

Irmi screamed after them, "Don't you understand? They won—we lost! The Bolsheviks are coming! The Nazis did horrible things to the people in Russia, and they will now do horrible things to us." Irmi ran to her bedroom.

Fritz felt a tremor of panic. How bad was it going to be? They could pack a crate with food, take blankets, and run to the hole. Fritz knew he could find it. Knowing they could all stay there safely might make Mama feel better. He decided to tell her.

Mama came down from the attic with a bedsheet from the chest of drawers.

"What are you doing now?" Fritz asked.

"We'll hoist this on the flagpole to show that we surrender," she said. Fritz looked at her face and knew that she had been crying.

"Grandpa Karl dug a hole in the forest. I know where it is. We can go there and hide until the Russians have passed," he told Mama hastily, imagining himself leading the family toward the hole under the forked tree. Mama looked at him, her eyes widened. She took several short breaths. The pause grew longer, and he saw exactly the moment she made the decision.

"No. We're going to stay here. Lech will stay with us. We'll show a white flag and hope for the best."

9

The sound of hooves on the cobblestone echoed from the street. From the back of the house the roar of a tank drew closer. Mama sat down between Irmi and Fritz on the sofa. Then Fritz heard shouts, and Mama grasped his hand.

Lech moved the curtains to look out the window. Fritz saw the white sheet flapping from above. He was glad that Lech was with them in the house.

"Just keep breathing, everyone!" Lech said and sat down in the chair by the window. "They will be wild and scary-looking. Do what they say."

Heavy footsteps sounded on the tiles in the hallway. Then three soldiers entered the living room. They all wore torn green jackets with small red flags sewn onto their sleeves. They shouted in Russian. Fritz held Mama's hand and tried to stay as close to her as possible on the sofa. One of the soldiers broke the glass of the sideboard with the butt of his rifle, took out the bottle of brandy, drank from it, and passed it to the others. They rummaged through the china cabinet, throwing the plates on the floor. Fritz saw the white china bowl break and little pieces of white porcelain with blue flowers spread over the carpet. Mama held his hand with a firm grip. Suddenly, one soldier pointed his rifle at them. "No!" Mama screamed. Fritz held his breath.

"*Stojat!*" Lech stepped toward the middle of the room, holding his arms up. The soldier turned to Lech, who spoke in what sounded like their language and motioned toward the pantry. The Russians seemed to understand. One soldier waved the tip of his rifle toward the door and motioned them to move. Fritz got up, holding onto a chair, his legs shaking. Following Mama and Lech closely, he walked into the hallway.

When they reached the pantry, two of the Russians grabbed sausages hanging from a hook. Others pried open jars of canned fruit. One jar broke on the floor, and Fritz watched four big gooseberries roll onto the black and white tiles, the translucent syrup magnifying the tile pattern. One of the soldiers ate pickles out of a jar; another slurped canned fruit. If they only wanted food, it might not be so bad. Lech handed them a sack and helped them fill it with jars, meats, and the dried sausage Oma Lou had saved for a special occasion. The soldiers stuffed it all into the sack and their uniform pockets, then, shoving Fritz aside, made their way to the door. Their boots echoed on the tile floor, and suddenly the house was quiet.

Mama let go of his hand, leaving a small pain where her fingers had clenched his.

"Irmi?" Mama screamed. "Irmi? Where are you?"

Where was Irmi? A minute ago she had been sitting with Mama and Fritz in the living room. The fear was still all over him, and another wave of panic crept down his shoulders. Had they taken his sister? Fritz ran back into the living room, his shoes crunching on the broken china. "Irmi?" She was not there.

"Irmi?" He heard Mama call from the yard. Fritz ran back to the kitchen. It also had been looted by the Russians. He scanned the room. The bread box was empty, and the intruders had left all the cupboard doors open. One drawer was removed from the sideboard, and cutlery was spread out on the table. The wooden boards they used for breakfast plates were scattered on the floor. Fritz hurried to the bedroom. He squatted to look under the bed, and there was Irmi, lying face-down, her arms covering her head.

10

When Fritz woke up the next morning, the house was quiet. Now it had finally happened. The Russians had come and left. The worst was over. He and Irmi had slept in Mama's bedroom. Mama still lay sleeping on her back, fully dressed, Irmi still clinging to her in her sleep. With a shudder he remembered the cold fear he had felt when the soldier had pointed his gun at him.

Fritz pulled his shirt off the chair and tiptoed into the hallway. The door to the living room was open. Illuminated by the morning light, the disheveled room looked less alarming.

They had cleaned up the kitchen last night before they went to bed. The drawers were back in the cupboard, and chairs stood arranged at the table. Fritz looked out the kitchen window. No Russians in sight. The only sound was the chatter of the chickens huddled together in the corner of the yard. What had the soldiers done to the farm? The door to the pigsty was open. His heart sank when he saw the empty pen. He went outside and walked swiftly to the horse stable, hoping to find Max's and Moritz's big heads nodding over their doors, but Grandpa Karl's two Holsteiner horses were also gone. Only Carino, the pony, remained. He nudged his lip at Fritz's shoulder. Fritz quickly rubbed the white patch on the pony's forehead and moved on to the cow stalls. With relief Fritz heard the sounds of mooing and chains rattling as he went closer to count the swishing tails. All ten cows were still in their places.

The garden fence was broken, and truck tires had torn through the garden. They had mowed down the gooseberry bushes, the rhubarb, and most of Oma Lou's lettuce and onions. With a sting Fritz imagined Oma Lou shaking her head and scolding the Russians for the destruction of her well-tended garden. At least the tomatoes were unharmed, and the rows of strawberries Fritz had planted stood untouched.

As Fritz walked back to the house. Lech came out of the barn.

"They took Max and Moritz and the pigs!"

"I saw that last night," Lech said.

"What are they going to do with all our animals?"

"Some they will use here. Others they will send to Russia," Lech said.

"Will the soldiers come back?" Fritz had not dared to ask Mama last night.

"Yes. They'll come back. Some of them might even set up camp nearby and stay for a while. We are now under Russian occupation," Lech said.

"How long will they stay?" Fritz asked.

"That's hard to say." Lech shrugged. "Once the Allies have taken Berlin, they will talk about what to do with Germany. But no one got hurt here. That's the most important thing." Lech looked around. "Is there any food left for breakfast, or do we have to eat milk soup from now on?"

"The chickens are still here."

"Why don't you close the front gate while I get some eggs?" Lech turned back toward the chicken house.

Before he pulled the heavy wooden gate shut, Fritz looked down the village road. Old Frau Bartel was sweeping broken glass from the sidewalk in front of her house. A military truck had parked in front of the pub. White flags—sheets, linen, and tablecloths—were hanging from the windows on both sides of the street. Just one house had chosen a different color. On the flagpole outside of Paul's family's house a red flag fluttered in the wind.

11

Irmi had already finished milking her five cows when Fritz put his stool down to the right of Bertha's rear end and placed the bucket under it. He massaged the cow's udder, took hold of two teats, and applied gentle pressure with his thumb and index finger, just as Oma Lou had showed him, letting the other three fingers follow one by one with a slight downward tug. The milk splashed down into the bucket. It was comforting to fall into the familiar rhythm of this chore. At least one thing remained the same—cows needed milking twice a day. Bertha turned her head, chewing her cud. When the bucket was full, Fritz poured the milk into the churn through a strainer.

"Here you are." Paul entered the stable, ducking away from Bertha's tail.

"I'm almost done. Irmi will work the centrifuge," Fritz said. "Did the Russians come into your house as well?"

"Yes," Paul nodded. "They came and broke stuff. They took my mother's brooch. I told her to hide it, but she was sure they wouldn't touch anything because of the red flag. She showed them my dad's Party book, but they didn't care. They shot one of the pigs right there in the middle of the yard. Then they took the rest, our goats, and Willi's rabbit. He cried all morning."

Fritz remembered their last conversation, when Paul had said that his family was looking forward to the arrival of the Russians. But he decided not to say anything. He didn't want to start another argument.

"Let's go and see what else happened in the village," Paul said as Fritz hung up his apron and washed out the bucket.

They walked down to the end of the yard and turned the corner, passing the barn. From there they could see down to the pond.

"Wow! Look at that!" Paul said. Next to the pond sat a tank.

"It looks like it's stuck in the sand," Fritz said.

They looked around, but the tank seemed to be deserted.

"Let's go and look at it," Paul said.

The tank was the color of kale. The treads were crusted with a paste of pebbles and mud. When they moved closer, Fritz could see that a lid, like a round door, on top of the tank was open. From between two small slitlike windows a cannon barrel protruded, pointing directly to the back of their barn on top of the hill.

"We shouldn't go too close. What if someone shoots at us?" Fritz said. "What if a Russian is still inside?"

Paul took no notice of Fritz's concern. He even walked a little faster and stopped right in front of the tank.

"Hello?" Paul called. But no one answered.

"What if there's a dead soldier inside? Or someone who is just waiting for us to get close enough?" Fritz caught up with Paul.

"We should climb inside, see what it looks like in there." Paul motioned to Fritz. "You first!" Fritz wanted to protest, but he was too afraid that Paul would tease him. With a pounding heart he pulled himself up from the top of the treads to the opening and slid carefully inside the tank. It was dark and cold. It had looked so big from the outside, but it felt small on the inside.

"Can you see anything?" Paul called.

"There isn't much space in here," Fritz answered. Strange letters were printed on a sign pasted on the side. Lots of black buttons and red levers stuck out of a metal board under the window slit. Beside the metal seat and behind the steering levers he saw a package. Its German label read "Additional food rations for tank crews." He picked it up, wondering if the food package had been taken from a conquered German tank. "Are you coming?" Fritz asked.

Suddenly Fritz heard voices. Through the window slits he saw two soldiers. Both men had rifles hanging over their shoulders. He panicked and quickly dropped the package. Through the two window slits he saw Paul running up the hill. Fritz jumped to the opening, pulling himself up, his fingers clinging to the rim, but when he stuck his head out, he looked right into the face of a Russian.

12

The soldier asked him something in Russian. When Fritz didn't move, the man grabbed him by the arm, pulling him out in one swing. Fritz landed on the treads. He had to hold onto the tank to steady himself. Below stood the second man, who stretched his arm out, seeming to offer help to climb down. Without thinking, Fritz took the hand of the stranger, who swung him to the ground. By then both men were smiling, and Fritz allowed himself to relax. The soldier who had climbed up first now let himself slowly down into the tank. The second man clapped Fritz on the shoulder and said something in Russian. He was still smiling, and Fritz could see that he was missing a tooth on his right upper jaw. His head was shaved, and a thick scar shimmered through the bristles.

The other soldier reappeared from the inside of the tank, throwing down the package with the German label. His colleague pulled a knife from his pocket and opened it. Inside were several smaller packages. Fritz recognized a brand of cookies. On the side were four small rectangular bars wrapped in foil. The soldier with the scar took one of the bars and passed it to Fritz. He took it, and with a nod from the soldier he opened the wrapping. Inside was a dark brown solid. The soldier also opened one of the bars and took a bite from it. Fritz lifted the strange bar to his lips and licked carefully. If the soldier was eating it, the bar could not be poisoned. Fritz took a small bite. "*Shokolatte*," the soldier said. This was chocolate? He had heard of it but had never tried any. The solid melted in his mouth into a sweet liquid, exploding a wonderful taste. He smiled back at the man.

The soldier finished his chocolate bar and gave Fritz another. Fritz looked up. Was this for him to keep? He wondered if Paul was watching them from behind the hedge near the barn. The soldier patted Fritz's shoulder, nodded approvingly, again showing the missing tooth with a big smile. The other Russian now climbed down from the tank with a wooden box. He lifted the lid and took out two metal egg-shaped objects with a grid-relief on the outside. Both men stuffed three of the metal eggs into their jackets and turned toward the pond. "Come! Come!" the man with the scar motioned. Fritz did not want to go with them. By now Mama might be worried, possibly already on her way to look for him in the garden.

"No, thank you!" he answered, returning the men's friendly smiles. "I have to go home now!" Fritz pointed toward the barn up on the hill. "This is where I live. I have to go back to my mother."

"Mother?"

"Yes!" Fritz answered, relieved that they understood him. He nodded to emphasize the meaning of the word. The blond man addressed his fellow soldier in Russian. The second man nodded and repeated, "Maama!" turning to Fritz.

"*Dawai! Dawai!*" the Russians said, laughing and pushing him toward the hill, pointing up to the farm.

Paul was waiting for him behind the hedge at the barn.

"What did they give you?"

"Chocolate bars," Fritz said.

"Show me!" Paul demanded.

"Here." Fritz pulled out the bar.

"You have to give it to me."

Fritz hesitated.

"You wouldn't have it if I hadn't sent you into the tank," Paul said, grabbing the bar. Fritz wanted to protest, but Paul had already unwrapped the chocolate and taken a bite with a wide grin.

"I have to go home," Fritz said and turned away.

13

Until the fences were repaired, Fritz's main job was to herd the cows. It was a warm, humid afternoon when he had set out with his family's cows to the green pasture behind the pond. Dark clouds gathered in the west announcing rain. As the first drops fell, Fritz sought shelter under a big oak tree. The ten cows had spread out on the grass, some lying down to chew their cud. The wind rose from the west, and the clouds moved fast. Fritz leaned against the tree, wondering if the rain would last, when two Russian jeeps drove onto the pasture. Four soldiers jumped out of the vehicles and ran toward the cows, clapping their hands, and herding them toward the road. Fritz wanted to scream, but the sound stuck in his throat. Instead he turned and ran. It was only a short distance uphill toward the house. "Mama! Mama!" he yelled, "Where are you?"

"What's the matter?" Mama asked, coming out of the barn. "Why aren't you out in the field?"

"The Russians are taking the cows! They're driving them away!"

Mama walked with long strides across the yard.

When she reached the brow of the hill, she began to run. Fritz sped to follow her. By the time they arrived at the pastureland, the cows were moving slowly down the road. "No! No!" Mama screamed, running toward the soldiers. One man turned around, yelled in Russian, and laughed. Fritz saw Mama passing the animals, spreading her hands in an attempt to stop them. But the other soldier pushed her away, patting the cows' rears to encourage the animals to walk faster. Fritz did not move. He saw Mama stumble from the man's shove, her face frozen in terror.

"Rieke!" the name of the lead cow darted out of Fritz's mouth. "Rieke!" he called, stepping closer. "Rieke!"

The cow named Rieke turned around and trotted toward him. Two of the Russians reached their arms out to stand in her way, but Rieke continued on her path. One man yelled in Russian, but the soldiers couldn't stop her. The other cows stayed with the soldiers, and they ushered them down the road. The Russians turned around, laughing, amused.

With rain dripping from Fritz's hair, Rieke nudged him with her warm nose. Mama had collapsed under the tree, burying her face in her hands. Fritz walked over to her, followed by the faithful Rieke, and put his hand on her shoulder. "It's okay," he muttered, his heart aching at seeing Mama hurting like this. She looked up at him, but her attempt at smiling showed her distress even more. She swallowed hard, shook her head, got up, and wiped off her clothing.

"Thank you, Fritz!" she said. "I wish the others had followed her." Mama sighed and took his hand and led the cow back to the barn. "Looks as if even the sky is sad that we lost our cows," she said, tugging his hand to emphasize the joke, but Fritz knew that she could not make light of the loss.

Back at the house, Mama told Irmi and Lech what had happened. Fritz didn't want to be there, especially when Irmi clasped her hands over her mouth and made it worse for Mama by crying. They still had Rieke, who could supply milk for the family, but there wouldn't be any extra to sell. He washed his hands and looked at himself in the bathroom mirror. What a coward he was. He should have stepped in earlier. He had rescued only one cow. He should have run between the men and the herd. He should have tried to call them all back.

In the hallway he met Lech. "It's not your fault," he said, as if he could read Fritz's mind. "The Russians are taking all the livestock, from everyone."

"I wish I had done more," Fritz said quietly.

"You did what you could," Lech said. "I'm going to the barn. Would you like to come with me to work on your dog?"

"No," Fritz said.

14

The following Saturday, when Fritz returned from milking Rieke, a jeep was parked in front of the house. Lech and Mama were standing in the kitchen with two Russians. Mama motioned Fritz to come closer. These men wore real uniforms instead of the ragged bulky green shirts he had seen on the soldiers he had met at the tank. The taller Russian stepped toward Mama, stretched out his hand, and said: "Mikhail Petrov." His head was not shaved like all the other Russians' Fritz had seen so far. Mikhail Petrov had a full shock of golden-blond hair and a square jaw. He looked like the handsome Aryans the Nazis had printed on their posters. How strange to know a Russian by name. "And this is Sergei Babiuk." The second man, short with thinning dark hair, nodded in Mama's direction but did not shake her hand.

Mama turned to Fritz. "This is my son, Fritz." Fritz didn't know if he should greet the men with a handshake. How polite would he need to be to Russians? Fritz couldn't take his eyes off Mikhail Petrov's chiseled face. The handsome Russian smiled at Fritz and said that he spoke only a little German: "*Ich spreche nur wenig Deutsch.*" The words came out in a soft melody. He pronounced the *ch*-sound in the back of his throat. Mama nudged Fritz and said in a hushed tone, "Don't stare."

Later, Lech explained that the two men were the commanders of the Russian army unit that had taken and secured the village and that they planned to set up their headquarters in the house for a while. "Headquarters? What does that mean?" Fritz looked at Lech.

"They'll stay with us," Lech said. "They'll sleep in your grandparents' old bedroom, and they'll use the living room as their office." Fritz looked at Mama to see what she thought of the Russians moving in. But just then Irmi entered the kitchen, and when she saw the two Russians, she threw her hands in front of her face and let out a scream. Mama put her arm around Irmi's shoulder and pulled her closer. "It's okay," she told her. Fritz was not sure what to think. They seemed less frightening than the first soldiers who had come into their house, but Fritz made himself remember all the things he had been told about Russians by his grandparents, his teachers, and speakers on the radio. But then again, the two soldiers he had met at the tank had even given him chocolate. He argued with himself back and forth, trying to figure out what he thought of them. He certainly didn't like them sleeping in Oma Lou's bed. Irmi was more definite in her opinion. As soon as the two left to bring in their gear, she shrieked, "You want us to stay in the house with *Russians*?"

"Irmi, they will stay downstairs. We'll keep our rooms upstairs. They seem friendly. And we don't have a choice anyway," Mama said.

"We should go to Oma Clara's! We should have left before," Irmi said.

"We have the biggest house in the village. So I'm not surprised they want to move in here. If that's the only sacrifice we have to make, we are lucky," Mama answered calmly.

Mikhail Petrov was taking an olive-green canvas bag out of the back of their jeep when Fritz crossed the yard. He motioned Fritz to come closer. He squatted down, reached into the bag, and pulled out a photograph of a boy and a girl, both about Fritz's age, with their father's golden-blond hair. "*Meine Kinder*," he said, pronouncing the *K* like a *Kh*. "Aljosha and Katja," he said, smiling at Fritz.

"Aljosha and Katja," Fritz tried to pronounce the names, pointing at them.

"Are they twins? They look the same," he asked.

"Yes, yes!" Mikhail Petrov laughed. "They are same." He circled his face with his hand. "Yes, same." He said a Russian word that Fritz didn't understand. It was probably the word for *twins*.

Fritz smiled and said slowly, "Twi-ins."

Mikhail Petrov repeated the word, and Fritz nodded. They shook hands, laughing.

15

The next morning, Fritz went to Paul's house. He wanted to tell him about the two Russians. Paul's little brother, Willi, let Fritz in. "Fitz is here! Fitz is here!" he shouted as Fritz closed the door behind him and followed Willi into the kitchen.

Paul's mother was sitting at the table with a man Fritz did not know. "Good morning, Fritz," said Paul's mother.

"Werner, this is Paul's friend, Fritz. Gertrude Friedrich's son. Fritz, this is Paul's father, my husband."

His cheekbones pressed through his skin. A small cut left a red line on his chin, and Fritz wondered if the man had just shaved his beard. He wore an undershirt, and his collarbones stuck out.

"Nice to meet you!" Fritz said and shook the man's bony hand.

"So you are Karl Friedrich's grandson."

"Yes. ... He is dead," Fritz said, expecting a word of condolence.

"I heard he got away before he could get what he deserved," Paul's father said instead, piercing his eyes into Fritz, who wondered what he could have done to make Paul's father angry.

An awkward silence filled the room. Then Fritz remembered what Paul had said about Grandpa Karl and the Nazis. He turned to Paul, who focused on the kitchen floor.

"I have to go back home right away," Fritz said without looking up.

"What did you do with the sign?" Fritz asked Mama, who was working in the garden.

"Which sign?"

"The sign we used to have in front of the house that said that Grandpa Karl was the head of the Nazi farmers in town."

"I put it in the attic. It's wrapped in an old potato sack, together with all the swastika pins and Irmi's Young Maiden uniform."

"Why didn't you burn it?"

"We didn't have time. And metal wouldn't burn anyway," Mama said. "I put it under the hood of the old sewing machine, the one that Oma Lou never got repaired."

"What if they find out that we were Nazis?"

"Everyone in the village knows that Grandpa Karl was the local Nazi farmers' representative. And your grandpa Karl wasn't the only one who wore the swastika," Mama said.

"But what about the Communists? Are they going to do something bad to us because we were Nazis?"

"Fritz," Mama sighed and wiped her forehead with the back of her hand, "we weren't Nazis."

"But Irmi ...," Fritz started to say.

"Irmi had to join the Young Maidens. You would have had to join the Hitler Youth as well. No one had a choice. You just turned ten at a time when it was all falling apart," Mama said, motioning him to come closer. "Don't worry. They have to rebuild Germany. They need people to farm. And that's all we do."

Fritz ran into the house and hurried upstairs. Mama's answer had not dissolved his worries. The wooden floorboard in the corner of the attic gave a dry complaint when he ripped the sack from under the hood of the sewing machine. He dashed downstairs and took the main entrance to avoid Mama's questions. In long strides Fritz hurried along the village road. When he reached the sandy path that led to the forest, he fell into a trot.

He found the fork-shaped pine tree right away. The rain had flattened the pile of dirt, but the hole was still there. Fritz threw the sack down, remembering his last visit with Grandpa Karl. Now he wished he had brought a shovel. With his feet he kicked soil into the hole, feeling calmer as he saw the evidence buried under layers of dirt.

16

Soon after, on a warm evening at the beginning of June, Sergei brought a crate of vodka and placed it under the stairs to the backyard. He also carried out two chairs from the kitchen. At first Fritz thought they would invite Lech to drink with them, but then three other Russians came, one of them with an accordion. The man with the accordion sat down and propped his instrument on his thighs. He began first to pull and then to push with both hands, and the accordion released its elongated sounds. The player's right foot tapped to the rhythm, and his upper body swayed with each pull. Another man with a harmonica accompanied the accordion's melody.

"Fritz, come and help dry the dishes," Irmi called.

"The Russians will get drunk tonight," Mama commented. "We'll have a noisy night."

"They're celebrating our defeat," Irmi said, shaking her head. "I don't like them."

"They won't stay long. And if we manage to get along with them, they won't harm us." Mama had remained firm in her decision not to leave the farm. Fritz did not mind the Russians as much as Irmi, who was constantly complaining about Mama doing "slave work" for the Russian soldiers.

Lech entered the kitchen. "That was a great dinner," he said to Mama and joked, "The Russians are good for something after all, but it looks like we're in for a long night. They want to celebrate their victory and the end of the war."

"Yes, we were just talking about that," Mama answered. "We should go to bed early."

The music grew louder, and one man began singing. His deep voice vibrated with a sad song.

"Why are they singing such a sad song if they are celebrating?" Fritz wondered aloud.

"The Russians have deep, sad souls," Lech answered, smiling.

Mikhail entered and said something to Lech, who translated, "He wants you to come outside and join them."

"Oh no, thank you," Mama answered, but the Russian stepped in front of her, swinging his legs straight together, let his heels clap, and bowed down toward her.

"*Bitte*, Frau Friedrich," he said in his Russian accent, drawing the last syllable longer than the first and pronouncing the *ch* way back in his throat. He offered his right arm to their mother. Fritz was surprised to see Mama smile as she put her hand on the Russian's arm and followed him outside.

"I'm not going!" Irmi called out, after the door was closed behind them. Lech hesitated for a moment, then stepped outside as well. "Come. Let's finish the dishes," Irmi said to Fritz. "I can't believe they are celebrating our defeat right here under our noses." Fritz focused on drying the plate in his hands. "It's so humiliating," she continued as Fritz tried to catch a glimpse of what was going on outside. "I wish Mama would not go there."

"Lech is with her," Fritz said, working faster.

"That doesn't make it better," Irmi said.

"What's wrong with one dance?" Fritz asked.

"She is dancing with a Russian!" Irmi said.

"What do you have against them?" Fritz had enough of Irmi's constant bickering about the Russians. "They are treating us well. They share food with us. Mama says that they probably protect us from burglars and looters. So what's wrong with them?"

"You just don't understand!" Irmi threw the dish-towel over the rack. "They occupy our country. They bring Bolshevism. You are just too young to understand!" She ran into the living room.

Fritz switched off the kitchen light. If they could not see him from the outside, he might be able to stay longer at his observation post. He would love to go outside, but he knew that Mama would send him to bed immediately.

The accordion was in full swing, and another man had taken over the singing. His voice was not as deep, and he could carry the melody to very high notes. Fritz saw Mama standing on the side with Lech, listening to something Lech was telling her. Their shoulders touched.

The instruments played a faster tune, and one soldier stepped forward into the middle of the yard. He had folded his arms in front of his chest and began to jump from one leg to the other. When the beat grew faster, the man lowered his body as if to sit on his haunches. Then he kicked one leg in front of him, keeping his balance by bending his other knee. The others joined in a circle around him and clapped their hands to the rhythm. The dancer lowered his body further until he was squatting close to the ground, balancing himself on one leg while throwing the other leg out in front of him. Fritz wished that the adults would leave a bigger space in their circle so that he could see the lone dancer. The melody picked up speed, and the man was still jumping from leg to leg. The men waved their vodka bottles at the dancer and offered him a swig. When the music finished, the dancer bowed to thank his audience, let himself fall onto a chair, and wiped his forehead before taking a long drink from the bottle.

Mikhail turned to the accordion player and asked him something. The man nodded and took up his instrument. When the melody began, Mikhail turned to Mama and motioned for her to dance. She put her hand on his left shoulder and his arm circled her waist. They began to move to the music. Fritz never had seen Mama dance. He looked at Lech, who followed Mama's every move. Sergei had been sitting on the chair smoking and emptying a vodka bottle almost by himself. When he saw the two dancing, he got up and shouted something in Russian. Sergei staggered up the stairs and opened the back door.

"Irmi!" the drunken Russian shouted. "*Dotschka*!" Fritz followed him into the hall and saw Irmi just coming out of the living room. Sergei grabbed for her arm, but she pulled away and ran up the stairs. Fritz opened the back door and called for Lech.

Lech stomped through the hallway with Mikhail hurrying right behind. Fritz heard the heavy attic door open with a screech. Sergei was stumbling up the wooden stairs. Mikhail and Lech followed him.

"No!" Irmi screamed before she slammed the door shut. Mikhail called "*Stoj! Stoj!*" and grabbed his colleague's belt. He pulled Sergei down the stairs, fiercely whispering something in Russian, his eyes dark with anger. Fritz pressed himself against the wall, breathing quickly. Lech opened the front door, and the two Russians stepped outside. Mama had also come inside, calling Irmi's name. When she reached the top of the stairs, she called, "Irmi! Open the door! It's all right now. He's gone!" Fritz heard the door open, followed by Irmi's cries of relief.

17

For the next few days Irmi acted as though she had been wounded in the war. She complained about headaches. During meals she put on a pained expression, and before bedtime she insisted on pushing a chair under her doorknob to secure her bedroom at night.

"Couldn't Lech just sleep inside the house with us and make sure nothing happens to you?" Fritz asked when he and Irmi were alone in the stable. "Would you feel better then?"

"He is going to sleep in the house soon enough," Irmi said and gave him the older-sister-knows-it-all look. He thought he knew what she meant, but he didn't ask to confirm it.

In the garden, it was time to check on the strawberries. Fritz had mulched them with a layer of straw to prevent the plants from losing their moisture, but now, as the June sun had begun their final ripening, he saw that snails had attacked the red fruit. Oma Lou had shown him how to put eggshells around the strawberries to fend off the snails, but this remedy had not worked.

The slimy creatures had climbed over the obstacles and attacked the strawberries. As Fritz sat on his haunches, wondering how he could protect his fruit harvest, Mikhail stopped at the garden fence.

"I'll show you a trick," he said. He walked back to the house and returned with a bottle of beer and several small plates. Mikhail placed a plate on each corner of the strawberry patch and poured beer into each one.

"Drink, drink," he said, pointing to a snail. Then he let his head fall to one side and closed his eyes. "Drunk, drunk, sleep, sleep!"

Fritz laughed.

"Are you wasting the good beer on the snails?" Lech had come out of the barn and stood now next to Mikhail.

"I think he said that it will make the snails drunk and then they will leave my strawberries alone," Fritz said.

"I could think of a better way to use beer," Lech said and held his thumb to his mouth, imitating the motion one makes when drinking out of a bottle. Lech had a short exchange in Russian with Mikhail. Both men suddenly looked very serious.

"The Russians are leaving," Lech said.

"The Russians are leaving Germany?" Fritz asked. "When?"

"No," Lech said. "Our Russians, Mikhail and Sergei, are leaving."

"You're leaving?" Fritz looked at Mikhail.

Mikhail answered with a slow nod. "We're moving into barracks," he said. Now Fritz saw that Sergei had parked the jeep in front of the back door. He was packing boxes and bags into the back. Mikhail stepped toward Fritz. "*Auf Wiedersehen*," he said. Fritz wondered if they would meet again. He shook the Russian's hand and followed him to the car with Lech. Mama stood on the back stairs. She wiped her hands on her apron before she shook both Russians' hands. Fritz watched the jeep as it left the yard. He remembered how conflicted he was when he first met the two officers. Now he was disappointed to see them leave.

When he entered the house, he passed Irmi in the hallway. "Don't look at me like that," she said. "It's not my fault they left." Fritz only glared.

18

Paul flung another nail at the rusty can on the old chair. They had taken refuge from the hot afternoon sun inside the barn. Fritz had finished telling Paul about the sudden departure of the Russians, but he didn't seem to care much.

"My dad says that the Communists will organize all farming differently soon," Paul said.

"How so?"

"Everyone will have the same amount of land, and farmers will share everything."

"How can everyone have the same amount of land?" Fritz asked.

"People like your family have to give up most of theirs," Paul said.

"What does that mean? *People like us*?" Fritz asked, feeling the same tightness in his chest he had experienced when he met Paul's father.

"Former Nazis, like you."

"I'm no Nazi."

"But your grandpa was. People like him brought on all the bad things that happened."

"My grandpa is dead. Why do you keep bringing him up? You never even said you were sorry when he died."

"They put my father in prison."

"My grandpa had nothing to do with your dad having to go to prison." Fritz picked up a nail and rolled it between his thumb and forefinger before he aimed at the can.

"Your grandpa organized the *Volkssturm,* and he wore the uniform on holidays," Paul said, his voice triumphant now.

"But he didn't hurt anybody," Fritz said.

Just then they heard steps outside the barn.

A Russian soldier came walking into the barn. He was alone, his green cap cocked to the right side of his shaved head. The man was whistling, and when he came closer, Fritz noticed his swaying gait. A bottle was sticking out of his left pocket.

"*Dosvidanya,*" the man roared.

The soldier looked around the barn, appearing to search for something. He walked slowly toward the old motorcycle that stood in the corner. It had belonged to Fritz's father, but nobody had used it for years. The soldier wheeled it from the corner and threw his leg over the bike, trying to start the machine. Once he realized that the motorcycle was not starting, he got off and motioned to Fritz and Paul, calling something in Russian. They didn't understand him, but it was obvious that he wanted them to come closer. The soldier pulled a small revolver out of his pocket and screamed something at them. Paul turned pale. Reluctantly, Fritz moved toward the soldier. His heart raced, and there was a sudden shiver in the pit of his stomach. What did the man want? The soldier kept motioning and called out to Paul. Fritz reached the motorcycle, and the soldier forced his hands on the handlebars.

"Go, go," the man screamed in broken German

"He wants us to push it!" Fritz called out.

Fritz pushed the motorcycle out of the barn. The Russian pressed his revolver into Fritz's back. Paul pushed against the back fender. Outside, sunshine painted the yard golden. The farmhouse threw a long, sharp shadow, and the sky was dark blue in a late afternoon glow.

They pushed the motorcycle out through the main gate and turned right. No one was on the street. The three of them moved slowly, the soldier taking an occasional swig from his bottle. When they reached the edge of the village, the soldier motioned toward the hill on the south side of the cemetery. They crossed the cemetery, and Fritz thought, *If he shoots us now, we're right here.*

Streams of sweat dripped down from Fritz's forehead. His eyes stung, and he tried to wipe his face but couldn't reach it without letting go of the handlebars. Finally, they arrived at the bottom of Lord's Hill, as it was known to the villagers.

"Up, up," the Russian yelled.

They pushed the motorcycle up the hill, the Russian stumbling behind them. When they reached the top, he shoved Fritz aside and swung onto the seat. With a scream of joy he let himself roll downhill. The Russian bumped up and down, stretching out his legs on both sides of the motorcycle, like a boisterous child. Once the machine had rolled out onto the grassy flat, he turned around and waved his revolver in their direction.

"He wants us to come down," Fritz said.

"I know. He's crazy."

"Come, come!" they heard the drunken soldier scream, and a shot from his revolver split the air.

"Let's go!" Fritz called to Paul, and they ran downhill.

Fritz picked up the motorcycle and began to push it uphill again. Paul again helped from the back. The Russian walked beside them, waving his revolver. Once up on top, the Russian again let himself roll down, screaming and laughing. This time Paul ran down the hill while the motorcycle was still rolling. Fritz followed. How much longer would they have to do this? He was thirsty now.

The Russian soldier took a swig from his bottle. As he motioned the boys to push the motorcycle back up, he stumbled. The revolver dropped into the grass. Paul threw the motorcycle into the grass and tried to run away. But the Russian reached for his weapon and pointed it directly at Paul. The man let out a deep growl, like a large animal. Fritz couldn't move, his eyes glued on the Russian, who kept the revolver directed at Paul. Suddenly, Fritz felt a jerk at his sleeve as Paul pulled Fritz between himself and the revolver. He felt Paul's fingers holding onto his arms from behind. Fritz stared at the Russian, who frowned, his eyebrows crawling toward each other like two black hairy caterpillars. They were standing like this for what seemed a long time. He couldn't feel his legs. Then the man bent his head backward and laughed. He lowered the revolver and stepped back. With his left hand he motioned toward the road. "*Dawai! Dawai!*" he called. Fritz felt his legs filling with life again, and he tried a step forward. The Russian stumbled away. Fritz turned around. Tears glistened on Paul's cheeks. "I'm s-sorry!" he stuttered.

Fritz just stared at him.

"I know I shouldn't have done that. I was just ...," Paul pleaded.

"You don't really care about me. You're not my friend," Fritz said. "Leave me alone!" Fritz picked up the motorcycle and pushed it back toward the road.

Paul had not shrunk. There was no bang. But it was like a balloon had burst and nothing was left but air. The horizon quivered in the glistening sun. The cobblestones lost their contour to the heat. The road lay empty. Fritz put the motorcycle back into the barn and walked down to the pond. Better not to see anyone right now.

He passed the garden and his ripe tomatoes. Later, he would harvest them. They would not disappoint him. He took off his shirt, pants, and shoes and stepped into the water. It grew colder the farther he moved from the shore. He walked out until he lost the muddy ground under his feet and sank down, holding his breath. When it hurt, he exploded to the surface and let himself float on his back. The emptiness stretched out inside of him, helping him to stay afloat.

19

Summer was a good time to be lonely. July had turned into August, and the harvest had begun. Fritz helped making hay. He ran between the fields and the house, transporting water and food. Most days they all stayed out until dark and went to bed exhausted. Fritz volunteered for any chores they would let him do. He even asked if he could help with the laundry on Fridays, a chore Irmi happily passed on to Fritz.

It was early September now, but the days were still warm. Mama made a fire in the low stove under a big aluminum pot in a small room adjacent to the pigsty, called the pig kitchen. The pig kitchen had a low ceiling, and the walls exuded the smell of washing detergent and boiled potato skins, an aroma that Fritz liked and inhaled with a deep breath. He took turns with Mama, first stirring the laundry in the hot water before pulling it out. When they twisted the wet sheets around the handle of their long spoons, milky water ran toward the drain in small rivulets. Their faces grew hot, and sweat dripped down their necks. Just as the last piece was fished out of the pot, they heard steps on the gravel outside. A man's voice called, "Frau Friedrich?"

"I'm in the stall kitchen," Mama answered through the open door.

When the three men came closer to the door, the bright parallelogram the sun threw on the floor filled with their shadows.

"Could we talk to you for a minute?" the oldest of the three asked. Fritz recognized only one of the men. It was Paul's father.

Mama stepped toward the door, wiping strands of hair from her forehead. "Fritz, go down to the lawn and hang up the laundry," she said. The three men followed her up the stairs into the house. Fritz turned toward the laundry basket and bent down to pick it up, but when he heard the back door close behind the visitors, he stood up again, leaving the basket untouched. The smaller of the two kitchen windows was open, and he could hear the scratching of chairs on the linoleum floor. He walked to the window, staying close to the wall, bending over a little bit to make sure Mama would not see him.

"We're here as members of the land reform commission," one voice said. "We want to inform you that the commission has decided on the basis of the new government's land reform decree to divide your property. Your land holdings exceed a hundred hectares. The commission has decided to allocate small pieces of land to new farmers and refugees."

"So you're taking away my farm?" he heard Mama ask. Her leaden voice broke Fritz's heart. He swallowed. They were taking the farm.

"We also order you to leave the district and to move at least thirty kilometers away from Schwartz. You may take personal belongings and a horse cart but no livestock," the man continued. "This decision takes effect immediately."

Fritz let his body slump against the wall. He heard Mama's pleading tone, but he couldn't hear her words. His blood seemed to have flooded his ears. Fritz imagined the three of them with a horse cart, pulling their possessions toward the west like the people in the treks. Who could they stay with? He rushed toward the stall kitchen, picked up the basket, and made his way to the clothesline behind the barn.

The sun was already very high, and a dark blue sky met the outline of the pond at the horizon. To reach the clothesline, he had to step on a wooden block he had rolled out from the barn. Mechanically, he took a large sheet out of the basket, threw it over the line, and then fastened each end with a wooden clothespin. What was Mama doing right now? Had the men left? He couldn't go to her before the chore was completed. Fritz bent over to lift another sheet, but what if she was sitting all by herself in the kitchen crying? Fritz sped up his movements, but the basket didn't seem to empty. What if Mama was so desperate that she … ? He dropped the laundry and ran back to the house, raced up the stairs, opened the back door, and rushed into the kitchen. His mother was with Lech, who was holding her with both arms. She was crying. Lech whispered soothing words into her ear. Fritz stopped at the door. Watching them embrace felt uncomfortable, but hadn't he waited for this? He tried to detect the feeling more precisely, but Mama turned around, her face swollen and wet from tears. There was a dark spot on Lech's shirt where her face had rested against his shoulder.

"What's going on?" Irmi asked as she came into the kitchen.

"The land reform commission was here," Mama explained in a hollow voice, wiping her tears away with the tip of her apron. "We have to leave."

Fritz expected Irmi to cry and become hysterical. Instead she remained quiet. In a sober voice she asked, "Where will we go?"

After a short pause, Mama said, "We'll go to Oma Clara's and see if we can stay in Sempow until we have a better plan."

"Can't we go somewhere else?" Fritz burst out.

"Do you have any suggestions?" Irmi asked impatiently. "We don't have other relatives."

"I do have an uncle in Silesia," Mama said. "But it wouldn't be a good idea to go east. He has probably lost his home as well. We don't have a choice. We need a place to stay. We can't be choosy now, Fritz."

"I'll get the horse cart ready. We can take only what Carino can pull," Lech said.

"Take only what you need," Mama said to Fritz and Irmi.

Irmi hurried to the bedroom, but Fritz was glued to the chair watching the hand on the kitchen clock move. He wished he could slow down time by walking toward the bedroom in small steps. "Take only what you need!" Mama had said.

In the bedroom Irmi was folding her underwear into the old suitcase she had pulled from the top of the closet. Fritz sat down on his bed. The frame gave off the noisy squeak that sometimes woke him up at night. After today he would not hear that squeak again.

20

The hardest part was to say good-bye to the house he had lived in with Oma Lou. Leaving Oma's home was like abandoning her for good. After he had filled his crate, Fritz entered Oma Lou's old bedroom and opened the door to her closet. Empty. None of Oma Lou's clothes were left. Mama had altered some of them for herself and had traded others with neighbors for things she needed. But there still was the faint smell of Oma Lou's soap. He inhaled and held his breath, hoping that somehow he could seal the memory of her smell inside.

"Fritz!" Mama called from the kitchen. But Fritz could not yet leave the room. He pulled out the drawer of the nightstand and reached in the back. Oma Lou had once shown him the small album of pressed flowers she had collected when she was a young girl. It was still there. She had told Fritz that the flowers reminded her of the village near the sea where she had grown up. Fritz opened the slim album to a page with a flat round flower on a long thin stem. In her pointy handwriting the plant was labeled "Buttercup."

"Friiitz!" Mama called again. He stuck the small book into his pocket and left.

Fritz walked outside, keeping one hand inside his trouser pocket, patting the flower album. He joined Lech and Irmi, who were waiting at the cart. He looked over to the garden. More cucumbers had ripened and hung from the trellis. Other people would now harvest the rest of the vegetables. He had packed the tomato seeds. Maybe there would be a garden at Oma Clara's.

When Mama closed the door, she let out a single deep sigh. She looked awful. There were lines of strain around her mouth and shadows under her eyes. Fritz wanted to run to give her a hug, but he didn't move for fear he would break out in tears.

Once everyone was seated on the cart, Lech passed Fritz the horse's reins. As Fritz stirred the horse out of the yard onto the village road, he thought of the refugee treks he and Paul had watched. Now he was also a refugee, his home not taken by an enemy force but by his own neighbors.

"We didn't say good-bye to Oma Louise and Grandpa Karl," Fritz burst out as they passed the cemetery. He turned around to look at Mama.

"I know," she said, calmly. "We don't have time. But we'll keep them in our thoughts always."

21

The closer they came to Oma Clara's house the tighter the knot grew in Fritz's stomach. The main road separated two parallel rows of flat, plain houses with high-tiled roofs above low ceilings. In front of Oma Clara's entrance grew a well-tended rosebush, its dark green leaves shining in the last rays of afternoon light. Lech opened the gate, and the horse pulled the cart into the courtyard. Fritz looked for Oma Clara's geese to come hissing toward the fence. One had bitten him once. But the pen was empty. The Russians must have taken the geese.

"Hello!" Oma Clara stepped out of the back door. She was a compact woman, her cheeks ruddy from lots of work outdoors. Irmi jumped off the cart and fell into Oma Clara's arms. "Welcome, girl!" Oma Clara held Irmi tight. Fritz stayed on the other side of the cart, avoiding the inevitable hug as long as possible.

"They took the farm," Mama said, and Oma Clara just nodded as if she had expected that to happen. Then the two of them embraced. Mama introduced Lech. He took off his cap and shook Oma Clara's hand. Fritz was watching her closely. It was important that she welcome Lech. Oma Clara smiled at Lech. Then Mama motioned Fritz closer, and he found himself pressed against Oma Clara's housedress.

"How are you?" she greeted him. "Did you see the empty pen? The Russians took my geese. I thought you'd be sad to hear that." The women went inside. Fritz wanted to inspect Oma Clara's farm. It was so much smaller than the farm they had left in Schwartz. Her barn could use a fresh coat of paint. Fritz counted one cow and two pigs. A rooster strutted around the manure heap. There was no garden.

Lech had begun to unpack the cart. They carried blankets and clothes to his new quarters, a small room adjacent to the stable.

"This is better than Schwartz," said Lech. "There's a little stove, so I can make a fire in the winter, and I'll have electric light." Lech pointed to the light bulb hanging from the ceiling. Fritz nodded, trying to put together a list of good things about Sempow. Lech squatted in front of him and grabbed Fritz's sleeve.

"Listen," Lech said, focusing his light blue eyes on Fritz. "We will make this work. Here we don't have to live with Russians. We won't be evicted."

"She has no garden."

"There is a lot of work waiting for us here. I'll need your help, young man," Lech said.

Fritz looked down. "Yes," he said quietly. "I just miss Oma Lou."

"I know," Lech pulled him closer. "But your Oma Clara isn't such a bad woman. You know what they say: 'soft nut in a hard shell'?"

"I'm not sure that's the way the saying goes." Fritz looked up.

"Yeah, yeah, excuse my German." Lech laughed. "But you know what I mean."

When Fritz entered the kitchen, Oma Clara thrust a handful of silverware at him. "Here, Fritz, make yourself useful and set the table."

She asked him to put a small rectangular wooden board for everyone on the table and then stacked several slices of rye bread in a pile in the middle of the table. Oma Clara unpacked a dried-out block of cheese and a small earthen pot that contained a white shiny substance. Goose lard—Fritz shuddered at the thought of his least favorite bread spread. "You don't like this, do you?" Oma Clara handed him the lard. "In times of famine the devil eats flies." She laughed.

"I had some refugees from the East staying with me just until last weekend. The Sielmanns wanted to go to the American zone," Oma Clara said while they were eating dinner. "They came from Königsberg with an accent so thick you could cut a knife through it."

"Where did they go?" Mama asked.

"Once they learned that the Americans kept Western Germany, they moved on. I'm not sure that it's possible to cross over into the American zone, but I wish them luck. They were so fed up with the Russians that they didn't want to stay. I guess in Königsberg they had seen a lot of grief."

"Are there any Russians in Sempow?" Fritz asked.

"Oh yes. They're everywhere," Oma Clara answered. "They're taking the railroad tracks apart behind the eastern forest to transport them to Russia. Sometimes they enter houses and help themselves to food and water. I heard from Beth Littman that they were drinking out of her toilet." Oma Clara laughed. "Erna Schmittke told us that they fried potatoes in her bedpan! They are like children!"

"Children with weapons and vodka," Mama said, giving Oma Clara a look that made it clear she wished to end this conversation.

But Oma Clara continued, "Their headquarters are now in Nirow. Johann Müller is their man here in Sempow. He is now the leader of the local Communists. Remember him, Gertrude?" Mama nodded.

"He went to grade school with me," Oma Clara continued. "His family used to own the mill, but he got all political and moved to Berlin. After 1933 he relocated to Russia. He is a true believer in the new system, speaks Russian and all." Oma Clara shook her head.

"I will have to talk to him tomorrow," Mama said. "We need to register and apply for land. I hope they will give it to people like us."

Mama's last words hurt Fritz. What kind of people

were they? Refugees? People whose farm had been taken away by their neighbors?

"You know my opinion." Oma Clara smeared another slice of the bread with the goose lard. "But you are so hardheaded that you had to stay with your husband's parents. If you had moved in with me after your husband's death, you could have spared yourself and your kids a lot of grief."

Mama's eyes begged Oma Clara to stop talking about this. Fritz wanted Mama to defend herself. He looked at Irmi, who focused on her bread.

Fritz was trying to compose a sentence to support Mama when Oma Clara said, "But like I said before: You can stay here as long as you want. We'll make do!" Fritz wondered if she really she meant it.

22

Fritz didn't want to spend time alone with Oma Clara. But in the morning of the next day she asked him to help her while Lech worked in the potato fields. They led the horse the short distance down to the creek where a neighbor had left fence posts for Oma Clara's new fence. Fritz didn't like the horse. For a draft horse he was too nervous. Every time the singletree bar jumped over a stone the horse's ears twitched with fear. He chewed his bit nervously, white foam frothed from his mouth, and sweat glistened on both his flanks.

"I got him new just last week," Oma Clara said. "The Communists gave him to me, probably took him away from some rich estate. He needs to get used to his new home, just like you." They reached the creek, and Fritz fastened the reins around a tree trunk. "Don't want to look a gift horse in the mouth, you know," Oma Clara said as she expertly fastened the ropes around the posts and tied them to the singletree. "You're a real chatterbox this morning," Oma Clara said, looking up. "What's the matter, silent one?"

Fritz shrugged. "Nothing," he mumbled, hoping she

wouldn't try to prod a conversation out of him.

"I think the logs are tightly tied now," Oma Clara said. "All righty, let him haul." Fritz took the reins and led the horse forward. With his pull, the lines between the harness and the posts tightened. The horse threw his head back and took one step forward.

"That's it," Oma Clara called. "Make him go on."

Fritz grabbed the reins tighter and pulled, walking slowly forward. But the horse didn't move. "We should calm him down first and then show him how to pull. I think he doesn't know what we want him to do," Fritz said.

But Oma Clara was in a hurry. "The only thing we need to show him is who is in charge. He's a draft horse." The horse's ears twitched nervously. Oma Clara stepped forward and snapped a switch over the horse's rear. With a quick movement the horse stepped sideways, and several of the posts slid out from the looped rope.

"I need your help with these loose posts. Just tie the reins around that tree trunk and come back here," Oma Clara called. Fritz could see the white of the horse's eye as it tried to follow his movements. "Here, hold this end," Oma Clara commanded, pointing to a post that had rolled aside. But just as Fritz bent down, he felt the strong kick on his backside, and he flew forward, landing on his face in the mud near the creek. For a moment he didn't know what had happened. When he lifted his head, his left buttock burned with pain.

Oma Clara came running. "Are you all right?" She bent over him.

"I think so," he said and sat up. But he couldn't put much weight on his left side. The pain stabbed through him as he stood up.

"My boy," Oma Clara said, "he gave you a real kickin'."

Tears stung in Fritz's eyes from the pain. But he would not cry.

"Can you walk?" she asked. He nodded. "Then you can work." Fritz walked back to take the reins. The horse pulled calmly now.

"I guess he just had to get it out of his system," Oma Clara said.

In the evening Mama came with a jar of cream as Fritz was going to bed. "That will be a big bruise," she said. "Does it hurt?" Mama sat down on the bed and applied cream to his bottom.

"Not anymore," Fritz said.

"That's a mean horse," Mama said, closing the jar. He was still lying on his chest.

"Are you all right?" she asked.

"I don't like it here. I want to go back home," Fritz said, his voice quivering into the pillow.

"This is our home now. I miss the farm in Schwartz, too, but we all have to make an effort to get along," Mama said.

"Is Oma Clara making an effort?"

"She has taken us all in," Mama said.

"But I don't want to live here." Fritz turned to face her. "I don't ..." He wanted to tell her how much he missed Oma Lou and the garden. How he wanted to be happy. How he wanted to not feel hurt all the time. But the pained look on Mama's face again made him stop.

"You'll have to get to know Oma Clara," Mama said.

"When is it going to get better?" Fritz asked.

"The bruise will take a little while," Mama said.

"No, I mean everything," Fritz said. "You said that things would get better after the war is over. But everything is just getting worse." He was fighting a salty taste in the back of his throat.

"Oh, Fritz!" Mama squeezed his arm. "The worst is over. From now on it will get better. We will make it work. Just give it a little time." Her eyes were teary now. She had told him that the worst was over after Oma Lou and Grandpa Karl had killed themselves. Now she promised again that everything would get better. He wanted to believe her.

"Don't you want to go out and find other kids? You should find a friend," Mama said.

"Not yet," Fritz replied, and turned toward the wall.

shot. Then he saw again the last glimpse he had of Mama before the tarpaulin was thrown over the back of the truck. He replayed these images over and over again. They accompanied the rhythm of his work.

The feeling of loss clenched him and would not let go. Another log split into two. Fritz tried to imagine where Mama was now, but he had no picture for the place she could be. Maybe they were close and would come back soon? Oma Clara said they probably had been taken to a military police station by the Russians. But what did she know? She should go back and ask more questions. When would he see them again?

The sound of splitting wood lessened the pressure inside. He didn't want the pile of logs to grow smaller.

28

Fritz hated how Oma Clara made helpless attempts to cheer them up. What could help? He felt numb, and all he could think of was the last glimpse of Mama. But the next morning Oma Clara was all business again. She sent Irmi out to milk the cows.

"What are you going to do?" Fritz asked.

"What do you mean?" Oma Clara collected the dishes.

"What are we going to do to get Mama and Lech back?"

"There is nothing else we *can* do right now." Oma Clara looked at Fritz. "It has happened to other people, too." She turned toward him, leaning with her back against the counter.

"What has happened to them?"

"They were taken away by the military police under a false accusation. That's all we know."

"And where are they now?"

"The Russians have them." She looked down on the kitchen floor. "And they might have put them in prison."

"In prison?" The thought of Mama behind bars cut through him. "But she is innocent," he said, his own voice sounding thin and helpless.

"It makes no difference."

"You only asked the mayor."

"The mayor is the only one we can ask." She sighed. "No one can battle the Russians."

"You cannot be sure! We've got to try someone else!"

"Fritz!" Oma Clara looked at him sternly. "I know this is painful for you. But we can't do anything else. We need to wait for the misunderstanding to be cleared up. Then they'll come back. In the meantime, we have to continue our lives."

"It's your fault that they're not back!" he screamed and jumped up, the chair screeching over the floor. "You could have asked more people or found out where the prison is."

Oma Clara shook her head. "My boy," she said, "they don't want us to know what they do with their prisoners. I wish I could explain this to you."

"You're defending them!" He beat the kitchen table with his fist.

"No, I am not defending them. I'm trying to explain to you that this is all we can do."

"It's your fault!" he yelled. "You didn't do enough! You didn't show them that there were no weapons! You could have gotten them back!" The words shot out of him in a hot stream, his face burning.

Oma Clara looked at him, concerned.

"It's all your fault!" he screamed, his body melting. "I hate you!"

"Fritz! My poor boy!" She tried to pull him closer, but he backed away.

"I hate you!"

"Fritz!" Her voice was stern now. "Look at me, Fritz!" Her hand reached for his chin, but he shoved her away. Oma Clara clutched his upper arms.

"Fritz!" She shook him.

Wheels of red and black spun before his eyes. He kicked against her shin. She stepped aside, and he kicked the air. She slapped him. "Fritz, come to your senses!"

The hot stream froze. It was quiet in the kitchen. He looked at her. She was crying.

"Come here, boy! I am sorry!" She opened her arms for an embrace.

"Don't touch me!" He pulled away and stomped into the cold hallway. When he reached his bedroom, he locked the door and crawled under the heavy down cover, and wished Oma Clara would just die.

29

I have to find Mama and Lech. I have to find Mama and *Lech. I have to find Mama and Lech.* The words spun through his mind all day.

The next day at lunch Oma Clara made another attempt to get him to talk. "Fritz, I know you feel a lot of pain," she said. "You are aching so badly." He didn't need her to tell him how he felt. He remained silent. Fritz listened to Oma Clara but would not speak to her. She asked him to sort the last potatoes. He sorted them mechanically, thinking about Mama and Lech. She asked him to clean the kale. He washed the leaves in ice cold water, his fingers bloodless and numb, thinking about what he could do to find them. He wished it was spring or summer, when there would be many more farm chores. Now, in the darkest, coldest part of winter they only had to tend to the few animals left, but no fieldwork could be done. He longed for the harvesttime, the bundling of hay. Even weeding the beet patch, a once dreaded chore, seemed better than sitting around the house.

Icy hail rattled down all day and forced him to

remain inside. The large tile oven that was built into the connecting wall heated only the kitchen and the living room. It was too cold in the unheated bedroom, and he had to be in the same room with Oma Clara and Irmi for most of the day. Now, after a silent dinner, she had told them to dress in boots and warm jackets to help with the slaughter of a pig.

"How dare she do this?" Fritz handed Irmi her boots and sat down on the bench to pull on his own.

"Dare to ask you to help or dare to slaughter a pig illegally?" Irmi steadied herself against the door frame as she put her foot into a boot. "She needs our help since she can't call the butcher or anyone else. I hope she doesn't get caught."

"How will she kill the pig without everyone in the neighborhood hearing that awful squeal?"

"I don't know." Irmi shrugged. "But I am sure she has it all planned out. The hail will muffle the sound and help to wash out all the blood." Irmi held the door open for Fritz. "We need to eat. Meat will help us to get through the winter."

Oma Clara had emptied one of the back stalls in the stable and piled up several bales of hay. Behind the wall of hay she had collected all the tools she would need and buckets of water.

They had slaughtered pigs in Schwartz every winter. After the first frost, when the meat could be cured and stored in the cold, Grandpa Karl had called the butcher, who would arrive in a pony cart with his tools. He would kill the animal, examine the meat for parasites, and cut the pig expertly into the parts needed for processing. Oma Lou, Mama, and Irmi had boiled some of the meat or made sausage. Fritz had been allowed to watch, and afterward he had helped to scrape the hair off the dead animal skins. That was all Mama would let him do. On such evenings they usually had a feast of meat and sauerkraut and potatoes.

The pig Oma Clara had hidden was small. She had tied its snout with twine to muffle its squeal. But when Oma Clara cut the pig's throat after placing a large pot under the spot of the wound, it still let out a shrill squeal. The bright arterial blood pumped out, and the pig grew silent. When the red stream turned thin and finally ceased flowing, she handed Fritz the pot. "Stir this so it doesn't jell!" Fritz stood for a moment with the pot in both hands. He didn't know if he was nauseous from the smell, the sight of his grandma gutting the pig, or the assignment to stir the blood.

"Start now. Once the blood starts to set, it's ruined and we can't use it anymore," Oma Clara ordered. Irmi gave him an encouraging nod before she walked over to an enamel bowl in which the intestines formed a bloody mass. Her job was to clean them for sausage casings.

Fritz set the pot down in front of a stool and began to turn the wooden spoon slowly in the blood. Someone must have traded the runt to Oma Clara. But what did she have to trade? And who would trade with her since that was illegal as well? No one could get permission for trading or slaughtering since all the pigs were counted regularly by the Russians. If he were still talking to her, he would ask her why she wasn't worried that the meat might be infested with a parasite. They could all get sick from eating bad meat. But he would not ask.

Fritz sat with his back turned to the women listening to the sounds of their work. Oma Clara would need to burn the carcass once all the meat had been removed. But there would still be evidence. She would make sausages, and she would cook the meat. Those cans and jars would be stored in the pantry.

He stirred the blood faster and stared at the red swirl in the middle of the pot. Then he turned the spoon the opposite direction, forming an eddy.

The plan took shape while he stared into the blood. He imagined how he would go to Mayor Müller's office and demand an immediate appointment. The mayor would receive him and listen. Fritz would tell him that he had some important information to trade. If Müller would tell him where Mama and Lech were, Fritz would tell him that Oma Clara had slaughtered a pig illegally, boiled the meat, made sausages, and hid it all in her cellar. He would trade Oma Clara for Mama and Lech. The Russians would come and raid the farm. Then they would take Oma Clara and return Mama and Lech.

30

The next morning Fritz woke up determined to do a
had planned. Oma Clara had gone to the Farn
Association office and would not be back before n
In the washroom he combed his wet hands througl
hair, making sure it was carefully parted. He chec
himself in the mirror and plucked lint off his jac
His arms stuck farther out of the sleeves than they u
to, but he looked respectable enough.

Winter fog wrapped the low houses along the vil
street in a gray haze. It blurred the outlines of the ro
and muffled the sounds of his steps on the sidewa
Fritz inhaled the cold, wet air as he swiftly made his w
to the mayor's office. He took the three stairs in one l
and knocked loudly at the door. No answer. He knocl
again, and a woman's voice called him to enter.

"Good day!" A woman dressed in a thick, bla
woolen sweater looked up from a desk in front of
window. "Who's here?"

"Hello! My name is Fritz Friedrich, and I need
speak to Mayor Müller." Fritz was pleased with t
firmness of his voice.

"He's not in." The woman's face was wrinkled, but her hazel eyes shone warm out of the creases.

"When will he be back?"

She shrugged. "I don't know."

"I will wait." Fritz had stepped closer toward the desk and was now looking for a place to sit.

"Well, if you have time, you can keep me company while I take a break from this boring paperwork." She nodded in the direction of a chair. The woman spoke in the accent of the people who had come with the treks.

"Are you from Königsberg?" Fritz asked.

She smiled and nodded. "You must have heard the accent before." She turned toward Fritz on her swivel chair. She wore a heavy woolen skirt that looked to be made from a blanket. She held out her hand. "I am the mayor's secretary. My name is Lydia Kolbe. Nice to meet you, Fritz." Fritz shook her hand and noticed the two wedding bands on her ring finger. Just like Mama, she wore her own and what was most likely the ring of her dead husband.

"What's so important?"

"I can't tell anyone but the mayor."

"You remind me of my boy," she said. "He would be twenty-five now. But he died in Russia." She paused for a moment. "He had the same sharp line running straight up from between his eyebrows when he was angry." Frau Kolbe looked intently at Fritz, studying his face.

"Why are you so angry?" she asked.

"I'm not angry," Fritz said, grabbing his knees with both hands and swaying back and forth on the chair.

"There are lots of reasons to be angry during these times," she said softly. "I'm often angry myself." A crow had landed in the tree outside the window. From where Fritz sat it seemed the bird was sitting on Frau Kolbe's left shoulder.

"I am angry that I had to leave my beautiful home, the place I lived all my life, my horses, my trees, my parents' graveyard, my fields, and that I was forced to come here. And of course, I am angry that my husband and my son died because the Nazis thought they could conquer Russia." Her voice was trailing and she swallowed. "Are your mother and father still alive?" she asked. Fritz strained his ears for the sound of an approaching car.

"My father is dead. My mother is alive. I live with my grandmother." *Maybe he should just leave and come back some other time*, he thought.

"Where is your mother?"

"The Russian military police took her." Fritz pressed the words out.

"And you want to ask the mayor if he can help?"

Fritz didn't answer. He looked down at the floor, focusing on the grain in the wooden floorboards.

"Let me tell you something, Fritz." Frau Kolbe leaned forward. "Look at me." Her face was so close Fritz could see fine blood vessels lacing the whites in her eyes. He squirmed in his chair.

"The mayor is the Russians' marionette. He dances on their strings. I'm sure your grandmother has come and tried to find out where your mother is. Even if the mayor knew where they take the prisoners, he wouldn't tell you."

"I have something to offer him—a trade." Fritz knew Frau Kolbe would explain why it wouldn't be right to turn in Oma Clara. She'd tell him what he already knew—that they couldn't run the farm without her.

"My boy," she said, touching his arm with her cool hand, "don't even think of doing that. You cannot trade with the devil." She nodded her head slightly, as if she knew and understood.

Fritz felt his whole terrible story aching to come out. He wanted to tell Frau Kolbe everything, how much he hurt, how much he longed for Mama, how he wished he could do something. How he was so mad at Oma Clara for not trying harder. How he knew that they would never trade Oma Clara for Mama but that he hoped they would anyway. How the pain was like a missing tooth that his tongue kept caressing. But if he opened the floodgate, he would dissolve for good.

He got up. "I'll come back some other time," he said, avoiding Frau Kolbe's eyes and quickly walking toward the door. He did not hear her parting words. He hurried down the stairs, eager to inhale the cold outside air.

31

The cow was a good listener. Fritz leaned against her, not worried about the dirt and the smell. He could feel the rhythm of her pulse on his cheek. His body rocked in the same rhythm through the swell of his tears.

The cow was warm and didn't move when the words broke out of him. She wouldn't tell anyone how he was ashamed of his plan to turn in Oma Clara. She wouldn't tell anyone that Fritz just didn't know what to do now. The pain had burst like a shattered ink pot, leaking black over him. Mama and Lech had been gone for three days now. He pounded his fist against the cow's side, leaving a dark stain on her coat from his tears. The cow just shifted her weight and whipped him with her tail.

Afterward, he was exhausted. Fritz lay down on the bales of hay. He pulled his jacket tighter and rolled onto his side, making himself small. He was thirsty, but he didn't want to go inside. He didn't want to meet Irmi, who would ask about his swollen face and red eyes. He couldn't be comforted.

He didn't know how long he had lain there when Irmi found him.

"What are you doing here? Are you sleeping?"

Fritz got up, put his jacket on the nail by the door, and mechanically began to move the manure onto a heap.

"Are you all right?" She stepped closer, but he pulled away.

"How long do you want to keep this up?" Irmi asked. "You will need to speak to Oma Clara again, eventually."

He shrugged. "You're not talking to me either anymore?" she said in her older-sister voice.

"I'm just tired," he said, too empty to talk. He stabbed the pitchfork into the dirty straw. Lifting the forkful into the wheelbarrow was harder than he remembered.

"Come on! It's hard for all of us. We have to stick together and keep up the farm."

"It doesn't seem so hard for Oma Clara," Fritz said, forcing the pitchfork into the next heap of dirty straw.

"Of course it is. She just wants us to go on. When Mama comes back, she'll be very happy and proud of us. Let's not make it harder for Oma Clara," Irmi continued. She picked up a shovel and began to help loading up the remaining piles.

"When Mama comes back ..., when Mama comes back ...," Fritz repeated her words quietly. "But when *will* she come back?" He looked at Irmi.

"Oh, Fritz." Irmi put down the shovel and walked

over toward him. He let her put her hand on his shoulder. "We don't know. All three of us hope for their quick return."

"But I wish Oma Clara would try harder," he said, moving just one step aside so that Irmi's hand slid off.

"No one can do anything," Irmi said.

"I don't believe that. Something needs to be done." Fritz lifted up the wheelbarrow and pushed it toward the barn door. "I can't stand just sitting and waiting."

Outside, he unloaded his smelly, steaming load onto the manure heap at the corner of the yard and hurried back into the warm stable. Irmi was shaking the fresh straw out over the floor, distributing it evenly.

"Soon we get to spend some time outside the house anyway."

"How's that?"

"A letter from the school administration arrived today. We'll both begin school on Monday," Irmi said. "It'll be good to meet some other kids."

Fritz hadn't missed going to school. Right now he couldn't even imagine mustering the strength to walk to the schoolhouse.

32

Fritz opened the gray notebook with the torn cover. Some pages had been ripped out. Fräulein Streblow, the teacher, had told them that due to a shortage in paper it would take a while until they would receive new ones. Fritz looked at the lines on the page, then up at the blackboard in the front of the room where Fräulein Streblow had written the first writing assignment on the board: "What do you want to be when you grow up?" All the men in his family had been farmers. He hadn't written for a long time, and the pencil felt strange in his hand. Fritz had to look at the wall chart with the cursive letters to remember how to form them. The boy next to him was writing quickly. He had already filled several lines. Fräulein Streblow smiled at Fritz encouragingly. Before time was up, Fritz wrote a few sentences on how he would become a farmer.

For recess the students went out into the yard behind the schoolhouse. Fritz unpacked his sandwich and watched the smaller kids draw squares in the sand to play hopscotch.

With a sting, Fritz remembered Mama. She would

have made a better sandwich than the dry one Oma Clara had packed. Mama would have accompanied him to school and would have had some encouraging words for the first day. But maybe Fritz was getting too old for that anyway. He could hardly remember the last time he had been at school. As he finished his sandwich, the boy he had sat next to came up to him.

"Are you new here in Sempow?" the boy asked. "You don't seem to know anyone either." The boy had curly red hair and freckles. He smiled at Fritz, showing a large gap between his two front teeth.

"Yes, I'm new." Fritz looked at his sandwich, wishing the boy would go away then.

"Where are you from?"

"From Schwartz."

"Where's that?" The boy spoke with the nasal vowels of the sea coast accent.

"It's about a day's trip south of here." Fritz turned sideways to show that the conversation was over.

"My name is Konrad, and yours is Fritz. I saw it on the cover of your notebook."

Fritz wanted to say something mean, like "Oh, so you can read," just to make him go away.

"We came from Danzig in a trek," Konrad said. Fritz suddenly imagined him on one of the rickety carts he had seen with Paul. Konrad was not smiling anymore.

"How long did it take you to get here?" Fritz asked.

"Three weeks. It was terrible. It was so cold. We had

to sleep outside, and we were hungry. Once, a farmer took us into his house and gave us soup. It was the most delicious soup I ever had." Konrad paused. "What did you write about?"

"Write about? When?"

"For the teacher. What do you want to be when you grow up?"

"I wrote I want to be a farmer."

"I want to be a railroad man like my dad," Konrad answered. "My dad worked for the Reichsbahn."

"Did he drive trains?"

"No. He worked in an office, but he knew a lot about trains. We used to have a big toy train at home in Danzig, but I couldn't take it with me. I could only bring my book with pictures of our trains." Before Fritz could ask more about Konrad's dad, the bell rang and they had to go back inside.

Back in the classroom, Fritz observed Konrad from the corners of his eyes. Konrad listened closely to everything Fräulein Streblow said and raised his hand to answer questions several times. How could Konrad muster all this interest in school? Fritz grew tired from sitting inside for so long. He was glad when it was time to copy down the homework and pack up.

Out in the hallway the boys took their rucksacks from the clothes rack. Konrad asked, "Would you like to come to my house this afternoon to see my train book? I live above the blacksmith's shop."

Fritz didn't know anything about trains. But he was curious about Konrad, who also had lost his home. Fritz hadn't met with another boy since he and Paul had pushed the Russian on the motorcycle.

"Yes, sure," Fritz said. Just an hour in the afternoon to look at a train book wouldn't hurt.

33

When Fritz opened the gate to the blacksmith's shop, he faced the broad backside of a horse. A Russian soldier was holding the wooden handle of a small noose that was tied around the horse's upper lip. Every time the animal jerked its head the soldier turned the noose and tightened its grip. Fritz shivered, thinking of the pain that must cause, being pinched like that on the sensitive upper lip. He stepped closer and noticed the quiver in the animal's flank. The Russian soldier smiled at him, pretending to salute by tipping his left finger to his cap. Fritz smiled back. The blacksmith stood over the fire in a leather apron, holding a horseshoe in the fire with long tongs. With a swift move he put the red-hot iron on the anvil and began to hammer. Sparks flew left and right from the glowing horseshoe.

"*Guten Tag*! Hey! We have a visitor!" the blacksmith said. "Aren't you Clara Lendt's grandson? What's your name?"

"Fritz."

"Nice to meet you, Fritz. What brings you here?" The blacksmith looked up quickly before he struck with the hammer again.

"I came to visit Konrad."

"He lives right above us. You have to climb up the stairs." The big man nodded in the direction of the back door. He turned around and cooled the horseshoe with a loud hissing sound in a bucket of cold water. Then, with a swaying gait he walked behind the horse and bent down to lift its hind leg.

At the end of the steep, rickety stairs was a wooden door. His knock was greeted by a "Come in." Inside, two beds were pressed against opposite walls and a small desk and two chairs stood under the window. Gray winter light on the desk surface repeated the pattern of the white curtains. A woman was sitting on one chair holding a piece of cloth and a needle toward the light. "Hello! Konrad told me all about you." Her accent was even more pronounced than Konrad's, but her voice was pleasantly low. Konrad ushered Fritz into the corner of the room and asked him to sit down on the bed while he knelt down to pull out a suitcase.

"I'm going to leave you two alone," Konrad's mother said. "I must go look after the blacksmith's wife. She's not well." She put her needlework in a small basket and wrapped her cardigan tighter around herself. "Nice meeting you." Fritz got up to shake her hand for a good-bye. "I hope you'll come back soon." When he pressed her hand, Fritz noticed that her skin was cool and soft, unlike Mama's hands that were always raspy and warm. This memory of

Mama made Fritz swallow hard, but he managed to smile at Konrad's mother and nod.

Fritz looked around the room. It was small and smelled damp. On a rack beside the window he saw socks and a woolen skirt put up to dry.

"In Danzig we used to have a nice big apartment, right in the center of town, with high ceilings and a big tile oven in each room. But we had to leave when the Russians came," Konrad said.

"What's in there?" Fritz pointed at the suitcase.

Konrad opened the lid. "The train book." Konrad unwrapped the book from sheets of waxed paper. The pages were brown, and the hand-colored illustrations showed different types of trains.

"I used to have this one and this one as models," Konrad said, pointing to two engines. Fritz looked at the pictures. He didn't know anything about trains. Some of the trains were red, others blue.

"This is the E 19. The Reichsbahn had only four of these. One day my dad and I are going to take that train. It travels between Berlin and Munich and can speed up to 180 kilometers per hour."

Fritz looked at the red engine and tried to think of a question he could ask. "What's this?"

"That's a photo of me and my dad." Konrad held up a black-and-white photograph of a younger Konrad standing beside a handsome man in a suit who was embracing Konrad with his right arm. The man's hand, resting on Konrad's shoulder, was delicate for a man's hand. Fritz couldn't remember his own father's hands.

"He looks very nice," Fritz said.

"He is," Konrad answered, looking down. "When he comes back, he can work for the Reichsbahn again. My mother says he will find work anywhere the trains go. We can move to another city when we are back together."

"Where is your dad?" Fritz asked.

"We don't know exactly. The Red Cross is searching its lists for his name. He must be either a prisoner of war, or he is injured in a hospital. I am sure we will find out more soon." Konrad sounded optimistic, but if his dad hadn't returned from the war by now, he might be dead or starving in a prison camp. Fritz knew how terrible it felt to miss a parent.

"Do you have a letter from your dad?"

"No, but I am sure he soon will write." Konrad nodded as if to confirm his optimism to himself. "What about *your* dad? You said you live with your grandmother. And where is your mother?" Konrad asked.

Fritz took a breath to tell Konrad his story.

34

"And then they closed the tarp, and the truck left. That's the last time I saw her," Fritz ended.

"Do you know where she is?" Konrad asked.

"No. We don't know where she is," Fritz replied. "My grandmother asked the mayor, but he had no information."

"But if you didn't have any weapons, it should come out soon that it was a mistake," Konrad said.

"That's what I thought, too. But other people have been arrested as well without any evidence. My sister heard that it happened to the baker in Revekow and to the woman who operated the laundry press."

Konrad wrinkled his forehead, as if he were thinking about a really hard question.

"But if she was taken to a prison, wouldn't there have been a trial first?" Konrad reasoned.

Fritz could not answer. It became too painful to talk about it. He was caught up in the image of Mama in a prison dress, her head shaved bald and her eyes large dark-circled caves. He swallowed.

"I don't know," Fritz said quietly. "I wish I could do

something to find out where they are. The mayor will be no help!" He didn't want to tell Konrad about his attempt to talk to the mayor. "My grandmother says we just have to wait. That's what adults always say. First we waited for the Russians. When peace came, things would be better, they said. But everything only got worse. We had to leave our farm, and then they took my mother!" Fritz felt hot. He looked at Konrad, reading his face.

"But the Russians in Nirow might know something. That's where they have their headquarters. You could go there," Konrad said.

"That would be dangerous," Fritz said. "And how would I get there anyway?"

"I saw the post bus passing through the village today. I'm sure that the mail comes from the city," Konrad said. "You could take a ride with the post bus and then come back by foot."

"That's a very long walk," Fritz said. "I wouldn't make it in one day."

"How about a bicycle?" Konrad suggested. "It would be cold, but as long as it doesn't snow, you could get there by bicycle."

"Do you have a bicycle?"

"The blacksmith has one. It's standing in his shop, and he rarely ever uses it. Since he repaired his motorcycle, he drives that whenever he has gasoline," Konrad said. "He lets me use his bicycle. I'm sure if I ask him I could get it for a day."

Fritz wondered if Konrad really believed that he could ride the bicycle to Nirow. Or was Konrad trying to talk him into something?

"Maybe I could go on Friday. Then I would miss school for a day." Fritz thought out loud. But he wouldn't commit yet. He needed more time to think.

"I could cover at school for you. I could tell Fräulein Streblow you are not well and take your homework. Then she won't contact your grandmother," Konrad said. "You should do it."

The plan was very tempting. "I'll think about it," Fritz said.

On his way home Fritz stopped at the pond. He put his backpack down and dug his cold hands deep in the pockets of his jacket. The gray, low winter sky reflected on the still water like a dark blanket. Lech had taught him how to skip a stone over water at the pond in Schwartz. Fritz imagined himself pedaling all the way to Nirow. Once he arrived, he would have to find the Russian headquarters and muster the courage to go in and demand to see someone with power. Tomorrow he would need to tell Konrad if he wanted to go or not. He felt that familiar ball of fear in the pit of his stomach, but Konrad had encouraged him. He thought Fritz could find out about Mama and Lech in Nirow. Fritz picked up a flat stone and skimmed it across the top of the pond. Lech used to say that if the stone bounced more than three times he could make a wish. The stone bounced four times, leaving a trail of ripples on the water's surface. Fritz closed his eyes and made his wish: *Let me find Mama and Lech in Nirow.*

35

Konrad delivered the bicycle to the meeting spot behind the church the following Friday. It was still dark outside, and the clear night had chilled the air close to the freezing point. A sliver of the moon gave off yellow light. "I'll make sure nothing will happen to the bike," Fritz said, wrapping his scarf tighter around his neck. Even with two sweaters under his jacket he was cold. He would need to pedal fast to keep warm.

Fritz entered the city limits at dawn. It looked as if little progress had been made since the end of the war. Most buildings stood in ruins, with their fronts bombed away. Groups of women, wrapped in what looked like several layers of clothes, stood on piles of rubble hammering stones or throwing each other pieces of debris. White clouds of breath billowed from their mouths. Their colored headscarves dotted the gray surroundings. Fritz stopped to ask one of them for directions to the Russian headquarters.

"Oh, the Ivan stays in the old residence," she said. "You need to cross the town square and turn right behind the city hall—or what's left of it."

The residence was a castlelike structure built in the last century by one of the county's dukes. Bullet holes speckled the walls, one wing of the building was burnt out, the roof had caved in, and scorched beams stuck out like pointy, rotten teeth. Fritz took a deep breath and got off his bike to push it closer to the entrance. *I can do it, I can do it*, he told himself. He had come this far. Now he would get inside.

"*Stoj*!" a Russian guard stepped into his way. The man asked him something in Russian. Fritz shook his head to signal that he didn't understand. He smiled and pointed to the building. "I need to speak to the commander." The man laughed, but not in a friendly way. It was more like the kind of laugh Mama would give when someone offered her a very low price for milk. The man walked once around the bicycle before he let out an approving sound with his tongue, pointing his weapon to the bicycle. Fritz's heart sank. If the guard took away the bicycle, it would cause great trouble for Konrad. It also would be very difficult to get home on time. Fritz couldn't let the plan fail already. He pulled the bike closer and said with as much confidence as he could muster, "I need to see the commander!" Fritz held the man's gaze, forcing himself to stand straight. The guard broke into deep, loud laughter, this time showing amusement. He nodded at Fritz, patted him on the shoulder, and motioned him to go.

With a sigh of relief Fritz pushed the bicycle onward.

He leaned the bicycle against a chestnut tree in the yard and entered the building. Inside, he stepped into a large vestibule. The tile floor was broken, and several picture frames enclosed empty spaces on the wall. Fritz walked up the lavish staircase. On the first floor a man stepped out of a door and asked him in heavily accented German where he was going.

"I'm looking for the commander," Fritz said.

"What do you want from the commander?" the man inquired. His brows pulled together into a hostile frown.

"I need to ask him something important." Once again Fritz tried to look more confident than he felt. On the man's shoulder pads twinkled two golden stars. A silver medal attached to a short striped band of ribbon was fastened to his shirt and swayed on his chest with every word. "Out!" The Russian reached for Fritz's shoulders, turned him around, and pushed him in the direction of the staircase, adding a stream of angry Russian words. Fritz stiffened his body and stood his ground as the Russian's fingers pressed into his shoulders.

"No!" he screamed. "I need to see the commander! Please!" The words came out louder than he intended, and the high ceilings gave them even more volume.

Suddenly a door opened, and another soldier stepped into the hallway. He looked at the scene and shot a disapproving gaze at the man who had pushed Fritz.

Fritz recognized him immediately. "Mikhail!" Fritz called. The man took a moment to focus his eyes on him. "Fritz?" he said. Then he asked in German with his heavy Russian accent, "What are you doing here?"

It was Mikhail, the Russian who had lived with them in the house in Schwartz, the man who had protected Irmi from the assault of his drunken colleague. Mikhail came closer and turned to the other Russian, uttering some stern words in Russian. The man left. Fritz felt the fear drop from his back.

"Come inside." Mikhail motioned him to enter. The room was a huge octagon, topped with a high ceiling decorated with stucco ornaments. A dark red velvet sofa stood in front of an ornamented balcony door. Fritz wondered where the duke and his family, who used to live on this estate, were now. Mikhail motioned him to take a seat.

"So what's the matter?" Mikhail made himself comfortable in the wing-back chair across from Fritz. His German had improved since he had lived in Schwartz. "Why were you screaming outside in the hall? Do you live in Nirow now?"

Fritz looked into the Russian's open face and began to tell how they had to leave Schwartz and about the day they took Mama and Lech.

36

". . . and the military police officer said they were in their custody," Fritz finished and took a deep breath. "Can you help me find my mother?"

Mikhail fished a pack of cigarettes out of his pocket. "I'm sorry to hear about your mother. If she had no gun, she will be free soon. If this was a misunderstanding, it will be cleared up quickly. The Russian system is just," he said tartly. The tone in his voice had changed. Suddenly, he seemed uncomfortable. He lit a cigarette, and they both followed the smoke with their eyes.

"You are the commander," Fritz said, his voice thin. "You must know where they bring prisoners."

"Yes, but I have nothing to do with criminal cases."

"But it's not a *criminal case*! It's a misunderstanding, and I need your help to clear it up!"

"No, Fritz. I can't help!"

"But you have to!" Fritz had leaned forward. On the desk he saw the photograph of Mikhail's children he had shown him the day Mikhail had moved in with them in Schwartz. "What if it was your children who didn't know where their mother was? Wouldn't you help them?"

A shadow moved over Mikhail's handsome face. He looked down at his cigarette. Fritz saw his Adam's apple slowly bob up and down as he swallowed. Fritz waited for an answer, but Mikhail only checked his watch. "I have to go. There's a car waiting to take me to a meeting in town." He stood to leave. "You need to wait. If they haven't done anything wrong, there won't be any reason to hold them. Just wait, and it will resolve itself."

"No, don't tell me 'just wait'! I don't want to wait any longer. I waited for a long time, and things got worse. You are the only person I know who could help us!" Fritz didn't like the sound of his voice. "You lived with us! You know Mama and Lech! We haven't done anything wrong! Why are you doing this to us?" His last words came out sounding as if his voice needed oil.

Mikhail bit his lower lip. "We do collect some prisoners in the basement of the next building. But they never stay long before they are transported to real prisons," Mikhail said in a somber tone. He walked over to the phone, picked up the receiver, and dialed. Fritz touched his cheek with the back of his hand. It felt hot. He took a deep breath, trying to calm himself.

"No," Mikhail said after her finished the phone call. "They're not here. That's all I can do."

Fritz got up to leave. He had a new plan.

37

Mikhail had said that they kept prisoners in the basement. Fritz walked along the side of the building, keeping his back close to the wall. He peeked around the corner. He could see the back entrance, but a guard stood leaning against the wall beside it. Fritz pulled his head back quickly. He waited for his heart to settle down before he took another look. It didn't matter now how late Fritz would return home. He had come this far. Now he had to continue.

The next time he peeked around the corner he saw the soldier walking over to the flat building on the other side of the yard. This was his chance. Fritz quickly ran to the back entrance and opened the door. Just as he stepped inside, he felt a pull at his shoulder. Fritz turned around. The guard had returned! The man lifted Fritz up with a swift movement and held him under his arm the way Oma Clara had held the pig halves. The man's turnip-thick fingers squeezed Fritz's side. Fritz squirmed and punched his fists into the man's padded jacket. He cried for help, but the guard's paw sealed his mouth.

The man carried Fritz inside and opened the door to a staircase that led down to the basement. With each tramp of the man's boot on the stairs, Fritz's heart sank lower. Would they lock him in the basement? Fritz tried to wriggle himself out of the man's grip. The stronger he resisted, the firmer was the man's clench. The Russian opened a wooden door and dropped Fritz down. Fritz staggered, and before he found his balance, the man nudged him deeper into the dark room. Fritz stumbled and fell, catching himself with his right hand. A sharp pain jagged through his right arm. Before he could turn around, he heard the door slam shut, leaving only a slim bar of light at the bottom of the door. He heard the Russian stomp back upstairs. Then there was no light at all.

The room smelled like mold and damp potatoes. Fritz sat up and waited until his eyes got used to the darkness. He closed and opened his eyes, but there was not much difference. He patted the wall around the doorframe, searching for a light switch, but could feel nothing, and the room remained dark. His right arm and hand throbbed. He sat down, his back against the wall, hugging his knees with both arms. What would they do with him? How long would he have to stay here? It must be dinnertime by now. If he didn't return the bike in time, Konrad would be worried. Oma Clara would be furious when she found out what he had done. But that didn't matter.

Fritz tried to steady his breath, but his body kept shivering. He didn't know if the shiver came from fear or the cold. The whole trip had been in vain. Even Mikhail couldn't help—or didn't want to. There was no more hope that he would find Mama and Lech. And now he was caught like a rat. Tears began to swell at the back of his throat. He swallowed hard. No, they wouldn't make him cry.

38

The door opened with a bang, and light shot into his cell. Fritz didn't know how much time had passed or if he had fallen asleep. He sheltered his eyes with his hand, but a shadow fell toward him and someone grabbed his shoulder and pulled him up. The man yelled a one-syllable word. Fritz tried to steady himself against the wall before he was dragged out onto the staircase where he looked up into the grinning face of the soldier who was tugging him up the stairs.

Upstairs, a group of seven men in uniforms were sitting around a dining room table. Long-stemmed candles dripped wax on a lace tablecloth. Bottles stuck out between white soup tureens and platters of potatoes and vegetables. Two men held their glasses in Fritz's direction and cheered as the soldier pushed him onto an empty chair. The men's flushed faces glimmered in the candlelight. One of them filled a plate with a thick piece of meat and set it in front of Fritz. He stared at the feast. Jars of pickles and marinated cauliflower stood together with plates of cabbage rolls. In one bowl Fritz saw chanterelles, his favorite mushrooms, which both of his grandmothers had kept in their pantry "for special occasions." The soldier who had taken him out of the cellar sat down next to him, added two potatoes to Fritz's plate, and nudged him to eat. Fritz picked up the fork. The meat was delicious. He had not eaten roast in a long time, and he chewed carefully, keeping his eyes on the scene around him. What would they do with him after they had finished eating and drinking? Drunken Russians were unpredictable. He remembered what had happened after the dancing in Schwartz. Would he have to spend the night in the dark cellar? Would they let him go? The soldier next to him spooned some melted butter onto his potato and smiled.

Suddenly, loud voices came from outside. The door jumped open, and the soldiers scrambled for their revolvers. Mikhail stood in the doorway. The soldiers straightened themselves. The room suddenly grew quiet.

"Come." Mikhail motioned Fritz to get up. Mikhail said something in Russian to the soldier next to him. He looked angry. "What are you doing here? I thought you went back home."

"I need to find my mother," Fritz said. "You said that you held prisoners in the basement."

"But I told you she was not here."

"I wanted to meet other prisoners to pass them a message." Fritz looked straight at Mikhail. "I need at least to get in touch with Mama and Lech."

Mikhail shook his head. "It is very dangerous. They could have taken you to prison as well," he said.

"Maybe I could have found them there." Fritz breathed calmly. He was not afraid.

"Let's go to the jeep," Mikhail said. The stern tone had left his voice. A soldier brought the bicycle, and Mikhail loaded it into the back of the jeep. "Get in. I'll take you home."

39

Oma Clara jumped up when Fritz entered the living room. Irmi screamed, “Fritz, where have you been?”

“I went to Nirow to the Russians’ headquarters.”

“No,” Irmi blurted out. “You wouldn’t dare.”

“Yes, he did dare.” Mikhail stood in the doorway. He walked over to Oma Clara and shook her hand. “Fritz is very brave!” Hearing Mikhail using that word to describe him gave Fritz a pleasant shudder. No one had ever called him that before.

“Mikhail is the Russian commander in Nirow now,” Fritz explained. “He is the Russian who lived with us in Schwartz for a short while.”

“Fritz is a very determined young man,” Mikhail began. “I can understand why he is so upset, and I am sorry for his ..., your loss. Unfortunately, it is not in my power to get his mother back. But I will see to it that your daughter sends you a letter so that you at least will know they are well.”

Irmi sat down on the chair. “I can’t believe you did this, Fritz.”

“When will the letter come?” Fritz asked.

"I don't know, Fritz. But I promise that you will get a letter," Mikhail said. "You know where to find me if it doesn't come." He held out his hand, and Fritz shook it.

"Thank you!" Fritz said.

"Thank you for bringing the boy back." Oma Clara shook Mikhail's hand again.

Irmi stepped forward. "I can walk him out," she said.

"I am so glad you're back, boy," Oma Clara said after the door to the hallway had closed behind Irmi and Mikhail. Her voice sounded soft, not angry. Oma Clara took one step toward him but stopped when he didn't move. "I want you to know that I love you, and your sister, and your mother. I miss her as much as you do."

Fritz looked at Oma Clara. She wiped her cheek with the back of her hand. He could tell that she was worried what he would do next. Oma Clara stepped closer, opening her arms. He embraced her.

40

Fritz shook soil off the carrot before he placed it to one side. Then he pulled another carrot out of the ground and adjusted the position of his knees to reach into the next row. He loved the smell of the moist soil. He would leave three plants standing untouched so they could flower and produce seeds for the following year. With his thumb he rubbed the dirt between his fingertips. At the edge of the garden the gooseberries had reached the size of small plums, their minute black seeds visible through the transparent gray-green skin. He needed to get gloves to protect himself from their thorns. Mama would make jam out of the sour fruit if there was enough sugar for canning.

Fritz woke up with a start. It was still dark outside. He tried to hold on to the warmth and sunny colors of his dream, but it was cold in his bedroom. Fritz dressed quickly. Even inside the house he could see his breath.

When he entered the warm kitchen, he was greeted by the delicious smell of doughnuts. "Good morning!" Oma Clara waved the wooden spoon, sending little drops of dough flying before she dropped a dollop of dough into the hot oil. She fished a doughnut out of the pot and placed it on a cooling rack. "Here, you want to help by sprinkling the powdered sugar over them? I traded goose lard for the powdered sugar." She offered him a sieve. He scattered the sugar over the shiny yellow doughnuts as she fried more of the yeast balls.

"Did you see what happened overnight?" Oma Clara motioned toward the window. A thick layer of snow covered the barnyard. "We're lucky that storm didn't knock out the electricity." Fritz put down the sieve to look outside. Small mounds of snow had gathered on the windowsill. "When spring comes, I will start a garden," he said.

"Oh, a garden is all pain, very little gain," Oma Clara said. "I usually just trade for what I need with Frau Bauer next door."

"But I am very good with plants," Fritz said. "I raise tasty tomatoes. We could sell them."

Oma Clara focused on the next doughnut. "Really?"

"The space between the stable and the water tank is the perfect place for a garden. Not too much wind and lots of sun," Fritz added.

"Maybe we can trade tomatoes for geese. Then you can also watch those."

He looked up at her, but she laughed and nudged him. "I got you there for a moment," she said. "Don't worry. No geese. Just the garden!"

Fritz sprinkled another shower of powdered sugar onto the doughnuts. He should have asked her earlier.

Just as he was wondering when it was time to try the first doughnut, he heard a knock on the door. It was Konrad, who had come to hear about the trip to Nirow. The boys sat down at the kitchen table, and Oma Clara placed the plate with doughnuts in front of them. "Grab them while they're still warm. I'm going to leave you boys alone so Fritz can tell you how he almost brought us all into the devil's kitchen by visiting the Russians," Oma Clara said, shaking her head at Fritz. Then she smiled and quickly mussed his hair before she left.

"He promised you a letter. That's good," Konrad said after he had listened to Fritz's account.

"Yes," Fritz answered. "But I wish I could have seen them."

"You're so lucky that you met that same Russian again," Konrad said. "I wish I had a promise of a letter from my dad."

Suddenly Fritz felt selfish and added, "Thank you for getting me the bike!"

Oma Clara had returned to the kitchen and set down a basket of firewood near the stove. "You haven't finished them all!"

"I'm stuffed." Konrad leaned back. "Thank you, Frau Lendt."

"Those were delicious, Oma." Fritz wiped the powdered sugar from his mouth with the back of his hand.

"Why don't you two go sledding? It's Sunday. No school. We have lots of snow outside, and there's a sled in the barn."

"Want to go sledding?" Fritz asked.

"Sure," Konrad said. "I love sledding."

The two boys passed the cemetery on their way toward the hill on the south end of the village, and Fritz suddenly remembered how, back in Schwartz, he and Paul had had to push the Russian on his motorcycle.

"What's the matter, Fritz?" Konrad said, looking closely at his schoolmate.

"Oh, I was just thinking of the day I had to push a drunken Russian up a hill on a motorcycle. At the end he pulled his revolver."

"That must've been scary," Konrad said.

"It was," Fritz said, and with the images of the scene, once again came the terror he had felt when Paul had yanked him between the Russian and himself.

How different it was to be with Konrad.

"We had bad experiences with Russians, too," Konrad said. "When we were on the trek, moving along the frozen beach of the Baltic Sea, we were attacked by Russian airplanes. They flew very low and shot at us. Since we were on a beach, there was no place we could hide. My mother screamed and pulled us under the wagon." Konrad took a deep breath.

The two stories lingered between them. Fritz and Konrad continued to walk silently. When they reached the bottom of the hill, Konrad also grabbed the rope to the sled and together they headed up.

41

The letter arrived two days later. It was a Wednesday afternoon as the three of them were sitting in the living room. Oma Clara was mending socks, Irmi was knitting, and Fritz was finishing his homework. Fritz knew it right away when the doorbell rang. He flew to the door and took the letter from the postman's hands. In the living room he handed it to Oma Clara. They sat down at the dining table, and Oma Clara began to read:

Dear Family,

We cannot tell you where we are held. But Lech and I are together. That gives us strength. Don't worry about us. We are healthy. There will be a trial, and as there is no evidence against us I am hopeful that we will come home soon.

Irmi and Fritz,

Please help Oma Clara as much as you can.

Love,

Mama

P.S.: Note from Lech: "Fritz should get the dog out of the wood!"

"Why is it so short?" Irmi asked.

"They probably can't write more. I'm sure if she could have, she would have," Oma said, and folded the letter back into the envelope. For a while they sat silently around the dining table. Fritz took the envelope and reread the letter, looking for more than the words said. Mama and Lech were together. They were healthy. Mama thought that they would come home soon. He let the words slowly sink in. It was good to hold the paper that had recently been in Mama's hands.

Then Oma Clara finally spoke. "I am so glad we got this note. Thanks to you, Fritz," she said, smiling. "I hope that she is right and they will come home soon."

"What does it mean 'get the dog out of the wood'?" Irmi asked. "We don't have a dog."

But Fritz had already gotten up and was on his way to the back room. He dressed in his quilted jacket and boots before going out to the barn, where he picked up Lech's carving tools and the piece of wood he had been working on. It still looked more like a pig than a dog.

Back in the living room, Fritz flattened a piece of newspaper on the table and placed the carving tools in a row in front of him.

"What are you doing?" Irmi looked up from her knitting.

"I'm going to work on my carving," Fritz said.

"In the living room?" Oma Clara asked.

"It's too cold in the barn," Fritz said, pointing to the

newspaper he had spread out to protect the table. "This will be a dog," he continued. "Lech showed me how to do it, and I want to finish it before they return."

Fritz picked up the carving knife and looked around the room. It seemed brighter than he remembered. He felt the warmth radiating from the yellow tile oven. In the corner stood the grandfather clock, its hands frozen forever at a quarter past four. How he had laughed when Lech had wondered if Oma Clara's sofa and chair were upholstered with an old brown poodle's fur. A small red stain remained on the wall from a bug Irmi had squished with a scream. A fine lace of spider webs hung between the windowsill and the Bakelite radio Oma Clara refused to switch on. This was the place where Oma Clara and Irmi shared his hope for Mama's and Lech's return. This was his home now.

Author's Note

This novel is fiction, but the background of what Fritz experiences in 1945 is based on historical facts and inspired by events of my father's childhood in East Germany. The Second World War, which the German Reich began in 1939, and the genocide that the Nazis pursued against Jews and other groups that the regime had declared racially inferior, caused widespread death and destruction throughout Europe. More than sixty million people died, among them more noncombatant civilians than in any other conflict in human history.

When the Soviet army advanced toward Berlin in the spring of 1945, their forays into German towns and villages were accompanied by looting, pillaging, and violence. Many of the soldiers wanted to take revenge for what the German army had done to Russians and other Soviet people during the invasion of the Soviet Union by Nazi Germany. The Russian and the German people had been indoctrinated with hate propaganda about each other by their governments during the war. Many inhabitants of the eastern provinces of Germany left their homes in fear of the Soviet army to flee westward on treks.

On May 8, 1945, the Second World War ended in Europe with Germany's capitulation. France, Great Britain, and the United States divided the western part of Germany into three zones of occupation, which in 1949 formed the Federal Republic of Germany. The eastern part of Germany between the Elbe and Oder rivers stayed under Soviet occupation. On October 7, 1949, the Soviet occupation zone became the German Democratic Republic, or East Germany, a socialist state that remained under the influence of the Soviet Union. The two Germanys were reunited in 1989, when the wall in Berlin and the border between the two Germanys opened.

After the end of the war the Soviet occupiers disassembled large parts of East German industry and infrastructure to send it to the Soviet Union as reparation. They also quickly installed a Communist government, working together with German Communists, some of whom had been in Soviet exile or in prison during the war. On September 2, 1945, Wilhelm Pieck, the leader of the German Communist party in the Soviet occupation zone, announced an agrarian reform, which expropriated all land belonging to former Nazis, war criminals, and farmers who owned more than a hundred hectares. Larger estates were converted into collective peoples' farms, and farmland was distributed among peasant farmers and refugees.

The Soviets maintained ten "special camps" in

their zone, several on the grounds of former Nazi concentration camps. Many of the prisoners were Nazis and war criminals. But due to the concern among the Soviets that National Socialists would continue their fight against them in an underground movement, an increasing number of innocent people were arrested, and sometimes only a whiff of suspicion or anonymous accusations resulted in imprisonment. About one-third of the prisoners did not survive the catastrophic living conditions in the camps.

My father was born on a farm in a small village northeast of Berlin, in what later became East Germany. His grandparents committed suicide before the Russians reached their village. At the time he and his sister were younger than Fritz and Irmi in my story, so they could recall only a few details. But they did witness how their mother was taken away at gunpoint. She spent four years as a prisoner in one of the Soviet "special camps."

My grandmother and aunt remained in East Germany, but my father left in 1961 to settle in the West before the wall was built and traveling between the two Germanys became more difficult. After 1989 I went back to the village where my father was born and interviewed several eyewitnesses of the Soviets' arrival and occupation. Most of their stories were more gruesome than the one I tell in the book. But there were also a few stories of friendly Russians who liked children and handed out sweets. An entire generation of Germans in the East and West who were children in 1945 grew up with the trauma of war in their families' history; many of them lost their fathers and their homes in the war. Although the Germans who were adults during the Third Reich can be blamed for supporting a racist, violent, and insane regime that brought on a destructive war of epic proportions, children were pawns in the events. They had to learn to live on despite their loss, grief, and fear. Fritz found a way to survive.

Most of the academic works and eyewitness accounts I have used are published in German and written for adults. For those readers who would like to learn more about the history of the Soviet zone of occupation, I recommend Norman M. Naimark's book *The Russians in Germany: A History of the Soviet Zone of Occupation, 1945–1949*, published in 1995 by Harvard University Press.